Don

His Defenders

Book 6

By

Ronna M. Bacon

Psalm 59:16.

Yes, I will sing aloud of Your mercy in the morning; for You have been my defense and refuge in the day of my trouble.

Deuteronomy 31:6 Be strong and courageous. Do not fear or be in dread of them, for it is the Lord your God who goes with you. He will not leave you or forsake you.

NKJV

Table of Contents

With a warm spring breeze blowing towards him, Don Devlin stood with his face raised to the sun and his dark brown eyes closed. He relished the warmth of the sun on his face. The winter was over and he was out and about on the walking trails near Lake Erie in his home area. He had planned to be further afield that day but God had not let him. Instead, he had felt that he needed to be near his home or thereabouts. He had no idea why.

Running his hand through his deep-red thick head of hair, Don stood for just a few more moments before he shifted his weight on his booted feet. He headed off down a trail, one that he had walked many times either alone or with friends. He was familiar with it but was still cautious. His head tilted as he heard singing. A lady's voice greeted him. Don frowned. This was not what he had expected to hear that Saturday morning but he shrugged.

Don paused as he stepped to the top of a rise in the trail, a hand resting against a maple tree coming out into the fresh green of spring leaves. He searched for the lady and not seeing her. He paced towards where he heard the singing, finding the lady at last.

Delanie Driscoll had escaped that day from what she considered the drudgery of her life. She decided that she was in a rut work-wise and wanted to change. She just didn't know what to do. Working as an advocate for handicapped youths was in itself rewarding but she was tired and ready to move on.

There were times when the illnesses that afflicted her young charges really drove deep into her. God was there with Delanie every day as she worked. She just felt burnt-out and ready to move on to something else. She just didn't know what.

A sound behind her had Delanie spinning, a hand to her throat. Her deep blue eyes widened in fear. This was not the first time that she felt someone near her. She had searched and even reached out to a friend to search as well. Doug, an ETF police lieutenant from Riverville, had gone over her house and her car. He could find nothing but did warn her. Her mahogany curls swirled around her face before her hands captured them. She stared at the tall, handsome man who stood nearby, not in a threatening manner but still alert and aware of his surroundings.

"I'm sorry." Don's white teeth gleamed against the tan on his face. "I didn't mean to startle you."

"That's okay. At least, I think it is." Delanie's brow wrinkled for a moment. "I just didn't expect to find someone else out here." Her hands tightened on the straps of her backpack. She didn't talk to men much and when she did, she felt uncertain as to what to say.

"Not a problem." Don studied her, seeing the apprehension and almost fear on her face. "Are you okay?"

Delanie shrugged. She didn't know how to respond to his concern.

"I guess I am. I just..." Her voice died away as she studied him closer. For some reason, she felt safe with him. *This is You, isn't it, God? You provided*

—

someone to make me feel safe and defended. I just didn't expect anyone.

"No, I don't think that you are." Don walked slowly forward to stand beside her. "I'm Don Devlin. I have a security team. And you would be?" His grin creased his face again.

"I'm Delanie Driscoll. And I am trying to convince myself to change occupations." She frowned as he continued to grin. "I disturbed you."

"Not at all. I heard your singing and didn't expect to find someone out here who might want a companion for a walk." Don waited patiently for Delanie to respond.

Delanie blinked and then stared at him. Was he for real? She didn't know him but felt safe with him. Her work had become dangerous for some reason.

"Thank you. I would like that. How far are you walking today?" Delanie rose, her walking stick in her hand.

Don shrugged. He had no real goal in mind. He just wanted to be out in God's country and relax.

"I have no idea. How about you?" Don grinned at her once more.

Delanie shrugged, her eyes searching the area around her. She felt unsafe now when she hadn't. Someone was out there.

Don watched her and then searched the area as well.

"You're afraid, Delanie. Tell me why. I have a security team and would like to help you."

Delanie stared at him, wonder in her mind. Had God just done that? Had God sent Don her way?

"You are? God sent you?" Delanie walked away, heading up the trail, knowing that Don had stopped and stared at her.

Don ran to catch up with her. He looked around, feeling someone close to them. He was suddenly afraid for the lady with him. His instincts honed over the years raised his awareness of danger.

"Delanie? What do you do?" Don's hand reached for hers, finding her tightening on his as he asked his question.

"I work as an advocate for handicapped youth. I'm in the process, though, of changing to something different. I just don't know what. Why would you ask?"

"Because you are in danger and I would like to know why." Don suddenly tugged her off the trail and to a hidden spot. A finger on her lips stopped her protest.

The pair listened as they heard heavy footsteps passing them and the muttering and cursing from the two men. Delanie's eyes were huge as she listened. This was not what she had expected of planned on that day. *Lord, where are You? Will You protect us from these men? I have no idea who these men are or why they would be after me. And Don is in danger as well. How do we get away?*

Don's hand kept Delanie in place. He watched the men walk back and forth in front of them before he looked around. He tugged Delanie with him, heading back towards the parking lot. Don shook his head as Delanie's mouth opened. She snapped it closed.

Standing near the parking lot, Don searched for the men. He didn't see them.

"Where's your car?" Don leaned closer to whisper in Delanie's ear.

"I didn't have it. A friend dropped me off and was going to come back for me." Delanie looked around. "That wasn't such a good idea, I guess."

"You would have had no way of knowing." Don's hand reached for her as he ran for his truck. "I'll give you a lift." He slid to a stop, his arm coming around Delanie as a van appeared in front of them. His hands rose as a man emerged from it, a weapon raised.

Forced into the van, Delanie sat as close to Don as she could. She could feel him tense as he prepared to defend them. Only, he never got a chance. The rise and fall of the weapon scared Delanie as it landed on Don's temple, driving Don down into darkness. Delanie screamed and then clapped her hands across her mouth. The weapon had been turned on her and threatened her with the same.

Chapter 2

Delanie's hand rested on Don's hand, trying to assess him while she kept an eye on the man. She had no idea who the men were or why they had attacked Don as they had. She could not see out of the windows, sitting on the floor as she was. The van bounced over potholes and bumps in the road, causing Delanie to fear for Don.

The van slammed to a stop, jostling Delanie and Don roughly. Her hand tightened on his, trying to find comfort from that. The van door slid openly violently. The man with them jumped out and then reached in with a grubby hand to grasp Delanie's arm. She was pulled from the van to the ground, stumbling to keep her balance. She stared in horror at the grubby hand with broken, ragged, and dirty nails that gripped her tightly. Pulled towards a house, Delanie struggled to stay on her feet. She was not allowed to look behind her. She could hear footsteps behind her but only two. Delanie was very afraid for Don and kept trying to turn and watch him.

She could hear two sets of footsteps behind her and snuck a quick peek back towards the van. Delanie drew in her breath sharply. Don was being dragged towards the house, his feet not functioning, and his head hanging down in a limp manner. It was obvious that he was not alert or conscious.

Delanie was shoved into the house and into an office. She spun, ready to run, her movements stilling as the weapon was trained on her. She stopped, her hands in the air. A quickly indrawn breath showed her fear for Don as the men continued to drag him across the floor and then just release their hands from his arms. Don dropped with a sodden thud to the floor, his eyes not opening, where he lay in a crumpled heap. Blood trickled down from the cut on the side of his head.

With her eyes on Don, Delanie didn't watch the men around her. She jumped as she felt a hand on her arm, yanking her backwards and into a chair. She lost her balance as her legs hit the chair and almost missed the seat. Delanie stared in horror as Don was dragged across the floor and then into another room. Her prayers became deeper as she prayed for Don and his safety. Her safety wasn't in her thoughts.

"Why?" Delanie spun to stare at the man standing near her. "What did he do to you?"

"None of your business. Shut your mouth." His hand raised as he directed a blow at Delanie.

Delanie's hand found her mouth as she felt the pain from the blow. Blood caused a coppery taste in her mouth. Her tongue found the cut on the inside of her lip. She struggled to control the tears that threatened to overflow.

"What did you do that for?" Delanie glared at the man. "What did I ever do to you?"

The man stared at her for a moment before he walked away, heading into the room to which Don had been dragged. Delanie was worried about him, not sure if she should try and walk after the men or just stay put. Staying put won. She didn't relish being smacked again.

The man who seemed to be in charge stood just inside the doorway to the room, watching Delanie. A grim smile crossed his face. He had fully expected her to be on her feet and following him but she didn't. He shook his head before he turned back to Don.

Don sprawled on the floor, not moving. The man walked over to him, a booted toe roughly turning him to his back. Don's arm flopped limply across his chest. A slight groan came from him. The man was frustrated. Don wasn't supposed to be hurt but he had been and that would not go over well with his employer.

Locking the door behind him, the man walked back towards Delanie, finding her on her feet and defiant in her stance. He stared at her, not sure what to do with her. Don was to have been on his own on the trail. At least, that had been the word that had come to them. He didn't like the fact that they now had a woman to deal with. His hand reached out as he gripped Delanie's arm tightly and then pulled her from the room and to another room. She was shoved inside and the door locked behind her.

Delanie spun to stare at the door, not believing that she had just been locked up. She spun in a circle, desperate to find a way to get back to Don. Her prayers began to raise and her fear lessened. She could feel the peace that only God could give starting to flow through her. Delanie curled up in a corner, her eyes on the door. She had no idea who the men were or why Don had been targeted as he was.

—

The man stood outside the locked door, staring down at his phone. His employer had sent a text asking if he had Don. He had no idea how to respond to him with the news that they now had a woman as well. He sent off that text, pocketing the phone before he walked from the house and to his vehicle. He drove off, leaving two men behind to watch the couple.

The men paced inside and outside of the house, watchful for anyone who was out of place. They had no idea why Don had been taken or why the woman had as well. It was not for them to do. They were just hired help, hired to keep Don from disappearing from the house.

Delanie paced the room, her eyes on the window. She watched as the sun moved through the sky, signalling the end of the day. Her phone was out as she stared at it. Delanie was puzzled. Why had they not been searched? It didn't make a lot of sense.

Don groaned as he rolled to his side, a hand on the side of his head. He stared at the bits of blood on his hand, not sure where it had come from. His head pounded as he moved slightly before his eyes closed. He drifted off into unconsciousness, not hearing the door being unlocked and one of the guards coming in to stand and stare down at him.

The man shook his head. This had been unnecessary, he knew. Don had not made a move to escape nor had the woman with him. He stared down at Don, wishing that things were different. Only they weren't. He had now become part of an abduction and that distressed him. The man turned and stared at the door before staring back at Don. He walked away, the door locked behind him before he began to walk away from the house and towards the street. He just kept walking, heading for his apartment and then for the bus station.

The second man searched for the other guard, not finding him. He stood at the door to Delanie's room, hearing her singing softly. He paused, the words that she was singing stirring old memories. Hymns, he decided, hymns that brought back his youth. He then moved to stand outside Don's room, troubled in his soul. Then, he too walked away and found his car. He sped off, not caring that the two were left on their own and that no one would be around for the foreseeable future. He just didn't care any more.

Chapter 3

With no cell service, Delanie just tucked her phone back into her pocket. She sighed to herself. This was not how she had planned her day. Her friend was aware that Delanie had hoped to find somewhere to spend the night on the trail and wouldn't worry until the next day. Delanie turned back to the door, a frown on her face. She walked quietly across to it, turning the knob but not finding that it turned. *Now what, Lord? I know that You are here with me and also with Don. How do I get out and away and get Don away as well? And he's hurt. He needs someone with him.*

Delanie found a blanket and curled up in a corner as far away from the door as she could get. She slept, not sure that she should be but she was. She was on her feet early in the morning, a sound awakening her. She stared around, disoriented for a moment.

Heading for the door, Delanie reached for the door knob without thinking. It didn't occur to her that it should not have turned under her hand. She walked from the room, heading through the house towards another room. Her feet took her that way without her thinking about it. Delanie paused at the door before she turned the door knob to it and then walked in, closing the door behind her.

The door closed behind her with the lock clicking shut. Delanie turned her head slightly at the sound but didn't think anything too much about it. She looked around, knowing that she had been directed there by God. She just didn't know why.

Delanie walked through the room, tripping suddenly on something that she could not see. She landed on her hands and knees, jarred by the sudden impact. She frowned, suddenly afraid. She could sense something off in the room and felt around. Her hand froze as she felt cloth and then a body.

"Who is this?" Delanie felt along the body, finding the face. "It's a man. I can feel the whiskers on his face. Who is this?"

Delanie felt the man's back, relieved to find him breathing. But that didn't explain why he had not moved when she walked into him. She felt along his face, pausing as he jerked back from her hand. She rested her hand on his cheek, trying in vain in the dim light to see why he had moved like that. She just wasn't able to.

Rising to her feet, Delanie searched the room, finding the small bathroom behind a closed door. She turned to stare back at where Don lay before she reached for a cloth and wrung it out under warm water. She was back on her knees beside Don, the cloth in her hand. She hesitated and then bathed at the wound on the side of his head. He tried to move away from Delanie but her hand just followed his movements. He lay still again, a sigh coming from him. Delanie was able to wipe away the congealed blood and assess the wound better. It seeped a bit of blood just from being cleansed. On her feet once more and back in the bathroom, Delanie searched for any first aid supplies. Finding gauze and tape, she was beside Don once more, covering the wound.

Don had not roused much at all from her care. That worried her. She sat beside him, a hand on his cheek, praying for him to awaken. She was deeply afraid, terrified more like it, she decided. And to be on her own in this situation? Delanie wanted out. She turned to frown at the door and then walked over to it. The door knob turned but the door didn't open. That puzzled her. It was locked once more and she could not understand that. It had been unlocked when she entered it. Who had been responsible for that?

Delanie paced the room, her arms wrapped around herself. She shivered in the chill before she was over to the bed and pulling the covers off of it. A blanket was soon tucked around Don. She frowned at his backpack before she covered it, managing to slip it off of him with a great amount of difficulty. On his back, Don didn't move even as Delanie tucked a pillow under his head.

Sitting as close to him as she could, Delanie's hand rested on Don's cheek. She was worried for her new friend. She snorted. How could she call him a friend already? She knew nothing about him, at least not that much. She did know that she trusted him and that was hard for her to do, to trust so quickly.

Her eyes grew heavy and she rose, finding a blanket to wrap around herself and another pillow. She lay down near Don, not wanting to be too far from him. This puzzled her for a moment before she drifted off to sleep. Her prayer was for her friend and his healing.

Don moved slightly a couple of hours later. He looked around through slitted eyes, his head pounding with pain. He sighed. He had no idea where he was or why. Don rolled to his side, raising his head slightly as he heard faint sounds. He frowned, realizing that someone else was in the room with him. His hand reached out to touch a body before he realized that it was a female. In his daze, he reached to wrap an arm around the lady, drawing her closer to himself. Don drifted off again, not having been aware enough to understand that he was held captive.

That afternoon, Delanie roused and realized that she had slept. She frowned as she felt an arm across her and holding her tight to a body. She shifted enough to stare at Don. He must have awakened, she decided, and rolled to his side. That didn't explain why he was holding her.

On her feet, she threw the blanket and pillow back on the bed before she paced the room. She stopped in front of the door, her hands clenching and unclenching. She reached for the door knob, withdrew her hand, and then touched it. It turned under her hand and the door opened. Delanie was hesitant to move forward, something holding her back.

She backed away from the door, watching as it closed again. She heard the lock click and then a vicious laugh before footsteps sounded on the hardwood floor. Delanie dropped to the floor, her hands over her mouth to stifle her scream. She moved closer to Don, her hand resting on his shoulder. She didn't know what was happening but she was terrified. *God, are You there? Are You defending us? Is that why I couldn't walk through that door? Your hand prevented that from happening. I don't know who was waiting out there but someone was. I fear for what could have happened.*

Don roused as he felt a hand on his shoulder. His head was clearer. He looked around, his gaze landing on Delanie. He frowned for a moment before he sat up, his eyes closing until his head cleared. He felt her jump as he did so but her gaze did come away from the door.

"You're watching the door. Is there a reason for that?" Don's voice was hoarse as he began to talk.

"There is. Someone keeps locking and unlocking the door. I opened it a few moments ago but God would not let me walk through it. It was then shut and locked and I heard someone out there. Who is doing this?" She looked over at Don, a frown on her face. "You're hurt. Why are you sitting up?"

Don stared at her for a moment, not quite sure that she was serious. She was. He shook his head and instantly regretted it. A hand landed on the side of his head as his eyes closed. He could hear Delanie saying something before her hand rested on his cheek. Without realizing what he was doing, Don leaned into it, finding comfort from her touch. That puzzled him. He was not one who dated, preferring the single life. That was, until now. He was drawn to Delanie and not just because they were in danger.

Delanie stared at Don, puzzlement in her eyes. She couldn't understand why he leaned into her hand. That was not what she had expected. She wasn't sure what she had expected.

"Why are you in here?" Don watched her closely.

"I wasn't in here to begin with. This morning, the door to the room I was in was unlocked. I knew where you were and found you. The door to this room was unlocked but it locked again after I was in here. Who is doing this?"

Don shrugged, not sure that what she said had actually happened. He just wrapped an arm around her and began to pray. He was afraid for his new friend and didn't know why.

Chapter 4

Don rose to his feet, swaying for a moment as he regained his balance. Delanie wrapped an arm around him to steady him. He stared down at her. He was tall himself, over six feet in height, but Delanie was tall for a lady. And a lady she was, Don decided, one who he wished to get to know and perhaps date. This was not him, he knew. *God, did You bring a lady into my life? I see my team and my friends and how happy they are with their spouses. You know the wishes and dreams of my heart. If this is You, thank You.*

He walked away from Delanie, the door to the washroom closing behind him. He stared at himself in the mirror, not liking the grubby look on his face. His head turned as he studied the bandage that Delanie had placed there. He could see the bruising on his face. Don sighed to himself. He was in rough shape, unsteady on his feet, and likely unable to protect and defend the lady with him let alone himself. With the water as hot as he could stand, he wiped at his face.

Back in the room once more, Don watched as Delanie paced the room. He frowned before he began a systemic search of the room. His hand rested on the door. Don understood what Delanie meant. He would not even try it. Someone was waiting for them out there and he would not go out there. He turned instead to the windows.

Delanie had paused at a window, leaning forward to peer out of it. It opened onto the porch at the back of the house. She turned slightly as she felt an arm around her. Don had found her, wrapping her into a one-armed hug.

"What did you find, love?" Don didn't realize that he had uttered an endearment. But Delanie heard it and then stared at him, wonder in her heart.

"This window. It opens to the porch. Can we get away through it?" She was away from Don, retrieving their backpacks, and was beside him once more before he could speak.

Don stared at her for a moment and then nodded. It might work, he decided, feeling along the frame. Then, he reached to raise the window. It went up without a sound. Don's hand helped Delanie through it and then handed out the backpacks. She took them, shouldering her own, and handing Don his when he slipped through the window and then lowered it. He looked around and then was over the porch railing, reaching to help Delanie.

The couple ran for the road and then across it, heading for some fields. They made their way through them, stumbling at times on the rows of dirt. Don paused at last, a hand to his head. It was pounding and paining but he refused to give in to the pain. Delanie's hand rested on his back as she searched the area around them. Nothing was obvious but she knew that could be deceptive.

Don reached for Delanie's hand once more and walked away from the tree that they had sheltered under. He had a vague idea of where they were but he just wasn't sure. He needed to find them shelter for the night and that might be an issue.

—

Delanie's fingers curled around Don's as she felt the strength of his character in how he held her hand. She too looked for somewhere to shelter. She had no idea where they were. All she knew was that they were out in the open somewhere and all she could hear were the sounds of nature. Not that she minded that but she would feel much safer if they were hearing the sounds coming from civilization.

"Don? Where are we?"

Don shrugged, not quite sure how to respond.

"I'm not sure. I'm just heading where God has told me to. He does that." Don shot her a glance even as he gave a quick grin. "By the way, what do you do for a living?"

"Me? I'm a paralegal and advocate for handicapped kids. What about you?"

Don rubbed at his upper lip, trying to hide his grin. She had sounded so fierce when she gave her job description.

"Me? Well, I run a security team." He began to laugh softly at the look on her face. "Yeah, one of those. You know? The people who protect others?"

"And you ended up like this? Who hates you that much?" Delanie's brows lowered as she thought that through.

Don sighed. Delanie had gone right to the heart of the matter with her words. Someone had been after him for months. The five members of his team had had adventures as they were termed as they struggled to protect the ladies in their lives. The five were now very happily married. But there had been something left over from all of their adventures. The men all acknowledged that someone was after Don and had used his team to get to him.

"I have no idea, Delanie. I have five men on my team. Each of them struggled with life and death situations when they met their ladies. Only there was something left after those adventures were solved."

"Someone used them to try and get to you." Delanie kept walking even as she struggled to understand that. "That's bizarre."

"It is but it happens. It did to two friends of mine with security team members."

Delanie stared at him, not quite sure if he was telling her the truth.

"Security teams? They're this good?" She smirked at him as his head shot around before he grimaced. "I'm sorry. I didn't mean to do that."

Don's hand pressed against his temple, willing the pain to stop.

"Yeah, they're that good. It's the other people who are the problem." Don stopped for a moment, shifting to remove his back pack. "We need to rest for a bit. Do you have any water or food?"

Delanie nodded, knowing that they did need water and food.

"We didn't eat for over twenty-four hours. We need to." She searched for a place to seat, her hand drawing Don over to a fallen tree trunk. She sat and Don found a seat beside her.

His head bowed as he began to pray, petitioning God to protect and defend them. Delanie's head bowed as well, her soft voice picking up his petition. Neither moved as they finished, the sounds of nature ringing in their ears.

Don looked up, seeing that it was starting to get late. He was on his feet, his pack on his back, and his hand reaching for Delanie's. They walked away, both searching for somewhere for the night. Don pointed at last. A ramshackle cabin appeared in front of them.

Don searched around the cabin and then inside before beckoning Delanie inside. He didn't dare light a fire, not knowing what the chimney was like. Instead, he pulled out aluminum emergency blankets and spread one out on the floor.

Delanie watched him before she reached for bottles of water and what food she thought that they could spare. She didn't want to put it all out, knowing that they would likely need some in the morning.

Don approached Delanie, sitting beside her and wrapping a second blanket around her. She stared at him for a moment, seeing the pain in his eyes but that his face was shuttered. She sighed. How did she get him to open up to her? *Lord, we're in this situation and I don't know how we are going to get away from the men and back to town. Please, dear Lord, guide our path.*

Chapter 5

Thomas walked into the office building on Don's property that Monday morning, a frown on his face. Don was usually there and ready to go before any of the five team members arrived. He turned as he heard the voices of Paul, Caleb, Joshua, and Mark.

"Thomas?" Mark appeared in the conference room, setting his travel mug on the table and looking around. "Don's not here?"

"No, he isn't."

Paul turned at that and then was running for Don's home. He tried the doors, surprised to find them locked. He pounded at the back door and then stood back. Paul shrugged at Caleb as he approached.

"I don't see his truck. He didn't send out a text to say that he wouldn't be here. At least, we don't have a team in today." Caleb's phone was out as he called Don. "It's going right to voice mail. When was the last that any of us saw him?" He looked around at his friends.

"Friday, I think." Joshua walked away, his phone out to call Don's sister, Daci. "Good morning, Daci. A question for you. Have you talked to Don today?"

Daci stared at the phone, not quite sure what Joshua was asking.

"Not since early Saturday morning. He didn't say what his plans were. That's not unusual. Isn't he there?"

"No, he's not. And his truck isn't here." Joshua walked towards the garage, standing on his tiptoes to look through the window. "His place is locked up tight and so was the office."

Daci stared at the wall across from her. This was not Don.

"Which one of you have keys?"

"We all do. One of us will head in and search the house. In the meanwhile, can you see if Aidan or Kaelen have heard from them?" Aidan was a police detective but a good friend to the men. Kaelen was also a good friend who had a helicopter service. "We might need Kaelen's help."

"We can't. He's away on vacation this week." Daci rose to her feet, pacing her office at the women's shelter. "Let me know what you find." She clicked off from the call, worry for her brother growing inside her. With what the other five men had gone through, they were all expecting Don to be targeted next.

Aidan walked towards the office building, finding Joshua waiting for him.

"Any sign of him in the house?"

"Not a sign. Paul and Mark walked through it. It looks as if he left it at some point over the weekend and just locked up and walked away." Joshua rubbed at his cheek. "This is not Don. He would just not show up without sending out a text to one of us."

"And he hasn't. Okay. What were his plans for the weekend? Do you know?" Aidan was puzzled at Don's disappearance. It was not him.

"Not really. He is quiet sometimes about his off time. And with what we went through? He's backing away to let us have time with our wives. We appreciate that but this? We need to find him and we don't know where to even begin to look."

"Was anything missing from the house?" Aidan looked that way, not sure if he should search it or not. "Let me walk through and see if there's anything off. I know you would have found anything but this may become a police investigation." Aidan walked away, leaving the five men staring after him.

Aidan walked through the house and then back out. He had viewed the security feed and saw Don driving away. He couldn't tell if he had anything with him. Don had accessed the garage through a door from the house. He looked around from where he stood in the back yard. Daci was almost running towards him.

"Aidan. Any sign of him?" She hugged her friend and thens stepped backwards. She had called their parents and both were shocked to hear that Don was not around. "Mom said that they had not talked to him since Thursday. That's not unusual."

"Not it's not. And no. Nothing. The only thing that we saw was his truck leaving on Saturday morning." Aidan stared down at his friend. "Do you have any thoughts?"

Daci shook her head, staring back at the house. A thought came to her and she ran that way. She searched through the mudroom and nodded. Don't backpack was gone but she didn't know if he had just gone on a hike for a day or if he had left for the weekend and found somewhere to stay Saturday night. She said as much as that to Aidan.

They turned as they heard a man's voice calling for Daci. Daci ran towards her father, swept into a hug before David turned to Aidan, a question on his face.

"Aidan? Any word?"

Aidan shook his head, knowing that David was there to help search for his son. He could see Deree, Don's mother, talking with the five men on the team.

"No. He drove away Saturday morning." Aidan walked away at last, troubled that his friend was missing. His phone was out as he searched his messages. He sighed. He was needed elsewhere. He just didn't want to do that.

Deree and David worked with the men, trying to determine just where Don was. They couldn't. The next week was spent with the team doing what training they had to with the team that had come in for that. Their off hours and then their weekend was spent searching for Don. They just could not find him.

Daci searched as well, putting out word on the street that she was looking for him. Don was beloved by those on the street. He never walked by one without a helping hand or a listening ear. He had shared many a meal with one or the other of them. The people had looked at one another and began their own search.

—

Kaelen walked into the office the next Monday morning, concerned that Don still wasn't home. He shared a look with Mark, who nodded. After an extensive time spent in prayer, the men split up. They needed to train the team that was in. Paul was free and walked away with Kaelen. Kaelen was intent on taking up his helicopter and searching the area. He had made arrangements to do that.

Disheartened, the two men stood by the hangar, deep in conversation. There had been no sign of Don. That worried them both. Paul's phone was out as he felt it vibrating. He stared at the text message. Don's truck had been found in an out-of-the-way parking lot by an officer from outside of their town. It was near to where Paul was. Paul simply responded and the two men ran for Kaelen's truck.

Chapter 6

David stood watching his son's truck as it was towed into the police department lot. He was afraid for his son. Where was he and was he hurt? He turned as Aidan and Toryn, the police chief but a good friend to Don, approached and stood beside him.

"Aidan? Any sign of Don?" David was hopeful that Don was there somewhere.

"Not a sign. I'm sorry, David. There was no sign of him." Aidan felt remorseful, knowing that it hurt his friend's father to know that. "We're planning on searching the trails in the morning. McKinley is going to bring in a search dog." McKinley trained dogs for security purposes and was Mark's brother-in-law.

"I see. I won't ask to go. I'll stay with Deree." David walked away, a discouraged and disheartened slump to his shoulders.

"He's hurting, Toryn." Aidan watched with sorrow and compassion as David stood by his car for a moment with his head bowed. "We need to find Don."

"He is hurting, Aidan. Like all parents would. And we do. We'll arrange the teams and head out at first light." Toryn walked away, disheartened as well. Don was a good friend to him and he prayed that nothing awful had happened to him.

The teams met in the morning and began their search. Even the dogs tried their hardest to find any scent. It was just not to be. Don's team stood around their vehicles last that afternoon, at a loss to know what to do. Richard, Don's lifelong friend and a fellow security team lead, and Abe who had another security team, had been there with their teams. Richard and Abe approached the men.

"He must be somewhere." Abe studied the area and then the parking lot. It was not the first time that he had to search for someone and wouldn't be the last, he knew.

"He is. Somewhere." Richard was hurting for his friend. He had prayed that they would find even the smallest hint or clue as to where Don was.

Mark shared a look with the other four on their team. They were planning on walking back over the trails again but with a team in for training, that would not be possible. Kaelen was planning of doing some flights over the area at the request of Aidan, a police officer with him to take evidentiary photos. They were at a loss.

The chiming of his phone startled Thomas for a moment. It was Don's ringtone. The seven men stared at one another before Thomas had his phone out. A text had come through from Don. They were puzzled at it. It didn't sound like him but it had to be him.

Guys, I need help. I'm not sure where I am. Can you track the phone? Delanie and I are out somewhere and I need to get to shelter. Only I can't find any.

The text had been sent that day. Thomas's shout brought Aidan and Toryn on a run to where they were standing. Aidan reached for Thomas's phone, shock on his face.

———

"You just got this?"

"I did. And it was sent a few days ago. Can we track it still?" Thomas thought that they could but he wasn't sure.

Aidan nodded, walking away with Thomas's phone. He forwarded the text to himself and then to the crime lab, simply asking that the tech try and track it. He returned Thomas's phone to him.

"Who's Delanie?" Mark asked the question that had been puzzling them.

"Delanie?" Toryn frowned. "I know a Delanie from town. She works as a paralegal. Is she with him?"

The men shared a look once more before they headed off. There was nothing more that they could do that day. Their wives walked into their arms as they reached their homes, hugging their men tightly. They had spent the day together and that day had been spent in prayer. Daci had been with her parents, worry about her brother uppermost in her mind.

David turned back from the door after letting Aidan in. Aidan had approached the house with apprehension in his manner. This was unlike him. The tech had tracked Don's phone to a place two hours north of them, on the shores of Lake Huron. Handing the coordinates to Aidan, he had stated that the message was at least four days old and he could not guarantee that Don would even be in that area now.

Aidan had nodded, tucking the paper into a pocket before he headed for his office. He was to have left already for home but had waited to see what the tech had for him. He sank into his desk chair, burying his head into his hands, praying for his friend. He didn't see Toryn pause outside his door before he entered and sat in front of the desk.

"Aidan? What did you find out?" Toryn spoke at last.

"The tech found out the coordinates but there are from at least four days ago. We can't track his phone so he either has it turned off or the battery had run down." Aidan studied his friend and boss. "Lyle was around. He wants me to head up that way."

"Take George with you. I don't want you on your own." Toryn hesitated. "Let me pray with you, Aidan. These investigations with our friends have worn you down."

"They have, Toryn. We prayed that didn't continue, but they seem to just keep coming. Who's next after Don?"

Toryn nodded at that. He rose at last, leaving Aidan staring at his desk before he was on his feet and reaching for his jacket. He needed to speak with David and Deree and didn't know how to tell them what he didn't know.

David pointed to the kitchen and headed that way. The family was trying to eat and offered Aidan a plate of the casserole that Deree had prepared. He took it with thanks, eating it and watching his friends as they attempted to finish their meal. He wiped at his mouth with his napkin before he spoke.

"David? Can we pray?"

David nodded, leading them in prayer. He sat for a moment with his head bowed, worry for his son uppermost in his mind. He looked up, seeing that Aidan was disturbed.

"Aidan? What can you tell us?"

"We managed to track the message that Thomas received. It came from a location north of us. I'm heading that way tomorrow. We don't know if Don is still there or has moved on."

"Our prayers are with you, son." David's hand rested on Aidan's arm for a moment. "I just pray that you find him and bring him home."

Chapter 7

Turning from the window in the motel room that he had finally found for them, Don studied Delanie. She was asleep, the bedspread pulled over her. They had walked for days, he thought, eating and drinking sparingly. His head was clearer and the pain lessened but he still had a residual headache. He frowned as he walked over to stare down at her.

Delanie had been a good companion, he decided, not complaining at all at the difficulties that they had faced. Fear had driven her to keep up with him. Reaching the edge of town, she had waited at a picnic table as he had headed for a coffee shop and returned with food for them. She had not flinched as he reached for her hand, seeming to welcome his touch. He was puzzled at that.

Don had studied her, knowing that he had to ask her a question, one that he had not thought to ask any lady. He bowed his head and prayed for her before he looked up. He wrapped her into a hug, finding her returning it.

"Delanie. We need to talk." Don's voice was hesitant, not his usually strong and confident voice.

"I know that we do, Don. It's not right, is it?" Delanie grew sober and sadness covered her face.

"It's not, Delanie. We've been out here alone for days now. I thank you for being such a good companion and trying to take care of me." Don hesitated once more. "Your reputation is important. I can't let anyone say anything wrong or hurtful about you. Will you marry me? I can offer you my name and protection until we get this sorted out. Then, we talk."

Delanie had half expected him to do that, to ask that question. She had prayed about it just as she knew that Don had prayed for her and for the situation. She didn't need to be told that. It was his character.

Hesitating for a moment, Delanie grew wishful. This was not how she had ever expected to receive a marriage proposal, if she ever did receive one. She turned her face to study him and then reach to hug him. Don was troubled by what he had asked, she knew that much.

"It's okay, Don. I understand." Delanie drew in a quivering breath. "We both need to guard our reputations. I accept your proposal." She looked up at him, seeing resignation in his face and then a look in his eyes that she could not read.

Don was on his feet, his hand reaching for Delanie. He looked around and then asked a passerby where the town hall was and then where to find a church.

Three hours later, Delanie stared down at the ruby ring that guarded the rose-gold wedding band. She had protested at that but Don had shook his head, his eyes telling her that he wanted her to have them.

Don turned from watching Delanie and reached for his phone. He had been able to get out a brief message to Thomas before his phone died. He had stopped at a store and purchased charging cables for both their phones. The phones were even now plugged in and charging. Don reached for his, finding it charged enough so that he could retrieve his voice mail messages and his text messages. He smiled slightly at how the tone had changed over the past few days. He had to decide who to reach out to but he wasn't sure which one of his friends or his family.

Aidan won the toss as he thought of it. He still hesitated as his fingers hovered over the contact number for his friend before he hit the buttons. Aidan's phone went right to voice mail and he sighed. He left a brief message before his thoughts turned to his team. There was a team in for training. Don hesitated once more and then reached out to Paul.

Paul reached for his phone, surprise on his face. Payton turned his hand to see who it was.

"Don?" Her voice was low.

"It is." Paul answered, hearing Don's voice ringing over the air waves. "Don? Are you okay?"

"I think so. I'm north of our town, Paul." Don turned as he felt a hand on his shoulder and wrapped an arm around Delanie. He hugged her to him with one arm. "I need transportation. No, sorry, we need transportation."

Paul stared at Payton just as she stared back at him. What did Don mean?

"Don? You're not on your own?"

"No, I'm not. It's a long story, Paul, and I'll explain everything once we're together. There's a lady with me, Delanie. We were abducted on that Saturday.

We've been wandering across the area to find shelter." Don bit at his lip, feeling Delanie hugging him. "We need to talk, Paul, with the team. But for now? Here's where I am. And tell the team that we followed Joshua and Jincy." He clicked off his call, the phone dropped to the desk in the room, and then he wrapped Delanie in his arms.

Paul stared at his phone once more before he looked at Payton, seeing the understanding on her face.

"He's married, Paul. He must have just done that."

"He would have, just to protect the lady." Paul sank back on the couch, Payton wrapped in his arms. They prayed for their friend and the lady in Don's life.

Setting up a group call, Paul hesitated as the men answered.

"Are your ladies with you, guys?" At the affirmative, Paul still hesitated to speak. "I just received a call from Don."

"Don?" Joshua expressed the surprise and then happiness of the team. "Where is he?"

"Up north. I think that's where Aidan is heading tomorrow." Paul turned to Payton, not quite sure now to continue.

"Is he okay?" Thomas was thinking of the health issues, being the paramedic on the team.

"He is from what he said. We didn't talk a lot. He did have something that he wanted me to share with you."

—

The men waited for Paul to continue, sharing looks with their wives.

"Paul? What did he say?" Caleb spoke for the group.

"The lady with him? They married, guys. I don't have much information other than her name is Delanie. I don't think that we can say much more to anyone as I don't know that he has reached out to his family as yet. I think he was hoping one of us would come and find them."

"And we can't." Mark was frustrated at that. "Didn't Aidan say that he was heading out of town tomorrow?"

"He is. George is with him so it has to be police related." Paul bit at his lip. "I'll reach out to him and let him know. He'll want to talk with Don before anyone else does."

David reached for his phone, answering it absentmindedly. He sat upright as he heard his son's voice.

"Don? Son? Where are you? Are you okay? We've been looking for you." Don's voice rose in volume and drew both Deree and Daci into his office, questioning looks on their faces.

"I'm okay, I think, Dad. I reached out to Aidan. He's heading to find me tomorrow. I'm sorry, to find us." Don bit at his lip again, not sure how to tell his parents what had happened.

"Son, we'll talk when you get home. But you said "us"?" Deree's voice reached through to Don.

—

"I did, Mom. I have shared an adventure the last few days with a lady. We married today, just because. Her name is Delanie."

His statement did not surprise his family. Daci looked thoughtful, her thoughts on the lady. She knew a lady named Delanie. Was she the one with Don? Her thoughts turned to prayer for the couple, asking God to defend and protect her brother and his lady.

Chapter 8

Walking through the motel parking lot the next morning, Aidan and George shared a look. Aidan had shared what Don had told him the night before with George. George had looked at him in shock, his mouth opening and closing without him saying anything.

Aidan tapped at the motel room door, waiting for it to open. He stared at the rough shape that Don was in as he stood back to let the two officers enter. Aidan's eyes narrowed as he took in the lady waiting across the room. He nodded. He knew Delanie and had worked with her at times. He just had not expected to find her with Don.

"Don? Are you okay? You look rough." Aidan turned to his friend.

Don shrugged, not sure how to feel. Delanie had insisted that he go to the local hospital and be checked out the night before. He had been, the physician telling him that he had likely had a concussion but was healing.

"I don't know, Aidan. Not any more." Don reached for Delanie's hand and drew her to his side. "Do you know Delanie?"

"We do. Delanie, are you okay?" Aidan turned to her.

"I am. Don was hurt and unconscious for at least a day. I made him be assessed yesterday."

"Thank you for that. Now, are you two ready to head for home?" Aidan waited for the couple to share a look. "We need to get your statements. Let's find somewhere to grab a coffee and then we'll talk."

Don nodded, reached for their backpacks, and followed George out of the room. Delanie's hand was tight in his. Aidan followed him, his eyes watchful. He didn't see anyone who seemed interested in them but he knew that could be deceiving.

An hour later, Aidan tucked away his notepad. He had been surprised at what had happened to them but he knew that he should not have been. George had listened carefully, taking his own notes. They would speak later, Aidan knew, and he would gladly accept George's impressions.

"Let's head out and get you back home." Aidan rose and headed for his car, the couple following him. George hesitated for a moment, feeling someone watching them. He couldn't see anyone who was obvious. It was just his years of experience as a police officer that told him that.

Don watched the scenery passing outside the car as Aidan headed back for Oak City. He refused to let go of Delanie's hand, finding hers clinging to his. They needed to talk but he prayed for his lady. He didn't want her harmed any more than she had been but he knew that was unlikely. He asked God to protect and defend them. His team would want to meet with them and that would happen on the morrow. Today? He needed to meet with his family and hers. She had not been very forthcoming when he asked her. That was a conversation that he needed to revisit.

—

Standing on his parents' front porch, Don thanked Aidan before he tapped at the door and then opened it. He led Delanie inside and then set their backpacks on the floor near the door. He walked towards the kitchen, squinting at his watch. It was near suppertime and he thought that would be where he would find his parents.

Deree turned as she heard footsteps, surprise and then joy on her face as she saw Don. She was over to him, wrapping him in a mother hug before she stood back to study him. She could hear David coming in the back door and stopping as he saw his son.

David too was across the room to hug his son, holding on just that little bit longer. He had worried about Don and now that Don was here, he wasn't sure what to say.

Deree turned her attention to the young lady who stood to one side, looking as if all she wanted to do was run away. She reached for her to hug her, finding Delanie hugging her back. Delanie had not expected that. She felt David's arms hugging her as well before Don reclaimed her, his arm around her.

"Mom. Dad. This is Delanie. She's my bride. We had to."

David and Deree recognized the little boy tone to their son's voice, one that he used to use when he wanted them to approve of what he had done.

"Welcome to our family, Delanie. We have waited years for you." Deree reached to hug her once more. "Now, do we eat first and pray or do we talk?"

———

"Eat, I think, Mom. And then we need to pray. We're still in danger. I just don't know why or from whom. And then we talk." Don turned to Delanie, reaching for her hand and drawing her into the kitchen. "We're not fancy, Delanie. We usually eat in the kitchen."

Delanie nodded. It was what she did when she didn't eat in the living room or at her home office desk. It was not a problem with her. She was just surprised when Don drew back a chair from the table, seated her and then sat beside her. His hand reached for hers once more. She was liking how her hand fit with his. She was just as sure that once the adventure was over, they would go their separate ways.

Daci paused as she shut the front door behind her, a frown on her face before she smiled. Don was here. She was in the kitchen, reaching to hug her brother as he rose before she turned to Delanie.

Delanie stared at Daci, recognizing her. She had not connected Don and Daci but then they had not talked much about their family. They had not talked much at all. That they needed to remedy and soon.

Daci watched her brother closely, seeing the care that he was taking of Delanie. She wanted to hear about their adventure but knew that they would be spending time in prayer before they did that. She was afraid suddenly for him and Delanie. This was not over for them, that much she surmised. And just what would they face?

Don raised his head when their prayer time was over. He turned to search Delanie's face finding her watching him. He gave her a small smile which she returned.

"Don? What can you tell us?" David's voice broke into his thoughts.

Don sighed, knowing that he had to tell them what happened to them. He was afraid for his family, knowing that whoever it was that was after him could very well go after his parents and sister. And there was nothing that he could do to stop it. He had no idea why or who.

"This is what happened, Dad." Don's voice filled the room with Delanie adding from her perspective.

The other three stared at them, not quite sure that they had told them everything.

"You have no idea who it is?" Daci spoke for the group.

"Not at all. I didn't recognize the men nor did Delanie. I need to investigate and I know the guys will be doing that."

"They will. They have already started, Don." Daci was sure about that, knowing the team and how they operated.

"They will have. I spoke with Paul last night and he was speaking with the team. We'll meet in the morning." Don looked around. "Do you know where my truck is?"

"At your home, son." David was on his feet, knowing that Don wanted to head for home. "Delanie

---

will want to stop at her place and gather some clothes and what not." He grinned at her for a moment.

"I would like that. Thank you for thinking of that." Delanie was on her feet, heading for the door, Daci beside her.

"It will work out, Delanie." Daci hugged her once more. "Don will do everything he can to solve this and protect you. So will his team. And his friends. He has many of those."

Chapter 9

Don paced his home late that night. He was exhausted but not ready to retire, if that made any sense at all. He rinsed out his mug and set it to one side, checking that the coffee was set for morning. Don knew that he was delaying retiring.

He walked back through the house, trying to see it from Delanie's point of view. He just couldn't. He would need to talk to her over the next few days.

Don paused at the open doorway to the bedroom that Delanie had chosen. He hesitated and then walked forward on quiet feet, to stand and watch Delanie sleep. He was on his knees with an arm wrapped around her, a finger wiping at the tears on her face. His prayer was raised for her. Don rose at last, heading for his own bed, hoping to sleep but instead spending the night in prayer for his lady. Delanie had begun to wriggle her way into his heart and he was glad. His dream had been to have a lady in his life. Delanie was the very image of his dream lady.

Delanie was on her feet early in the morning, disoriented for a moment. She reached for her phone, changing the voice mail at her office. She knew that there were would a lot of messages and emails waiting for her. Delanie just wasn't in the mood for that. She just wanted to be where Don was and that puzzled her.

Watching Delanie work in the kitchen preparing a meal for them, Don's eyes raised to the ceiling as he prayed for his lady, once more asking for protection and defense for her. He walked over to her and

—

wrapped her into a hug. She struggled to turn to face him, wrapping her arms around him.

Delanie had to admit that Don had scared her the week before. They had ended up staying in that cabin for at least four days. She had been unable to really rouse him except for once in a while when she had been able to get him on his feet. Delanie had managed to start a fire in the fireplace, surprised that the chimney was not blocked. She had searched for water and purified it with the tablets that she found in Don's pack.

Four days later, Don was on his feet, as unsteady as it was. He had nodded when Delanie asked if he was ready to move away from the cabin. She wrapped an arm around him to help keep him on his feet. They walked away from the cabin, heading for civilization they hoped. Arriving in town, they had found a meal, a motel, and married. Delanie was still uncertain about that.

"What's on for the day, Don?" Delanie leaned back to look up at him. She wanted to wander his property, to understand the buildings, and exactly what he did.

"My team is coming in this morning. Their wives are with them." Don smiled down at her. "I finally get to say that my wife will be part of the group." Without thinking, he dropped a kiss on her forehead.

Delanie stared up at him, taken aback by his gesture. She frowned, not quite understanding that

Don was staking his claim on her and that he would not willingly let her walk away.

"Don? How do we do this?"

"Do this? Us being married? It will work out. Joshua and Jincy were forced to marry. They are very much in love, sweetheart. We walk forward hand in hand with one another and with God as our Defender and Protector and live our lives. We are not out of danger. That much is clear."

"I know." Delanie walked away from Don to set their food on the table. "I need to get my car, Don. I have to go into the office at some point."

"We'll get it. If I don't get you to it, one of the ladies will. We look after one another, Delanie."

"I see. I'm not used to that, you know."

"No, you've said that." Don paused, not sure how to continue. "We never talked about your family. You met my parents and sister last night."

"My family? They're up in the Northwest Territories. That's where I'm from. I wanted to live somewhere else and they didn't like it. We had limited contact. In fact, I haven't spoken to my parents in years. My sister and brother just followed their lead and cut contact with me. Not that we were really close at any time. It's almost as if I wasn't part of the family. I certainly didn't look like any of them."

"You don't? Let me have their information. I have a friend who will investigate it for us. Emma does that for her friends at no charge."

"She does?" Delanie frowned at him even as she heard a tap at the back door and a couple entered. She frowned at them two, drawing grins from them both.

"Don?" Mark's voice drew Don's attention away from Delanie. "Care to introduce us?"

Mark and McKala moved forward to greet Don's bride. McKala hugged her, finding Delanie hugging her back.

"I know you from church, Delanie." McKala was happy to say that.

"You do. From our Bible study." Delanie bit at her lip. "And the other ladies? I didn't realize that you were all connected to Don."

"We are. Payton, Taran, Jincy, and Cullea are part of our group. We don't know you as well as we would like to. We also meet on our own for prayer and Bible study. Our guys need that backing from us. You need to join us." McKala simply reached to help Delanie with the final preparation of their meal.

Mark moved Don away, a question on his face.

"Don? How are you? I can see that you were wounded." Mark pointed to the healing wound on Don's temple.

"I'm getting there. We need to speak, Mark, and then get organized.

" We did start an investigation but we need to get Delanie's information as well. What does she do for a living?"

"She's a paralegal and advocates for handicapped kids. She is also from the Northwest Territories and is estranged from her parents and her siblings." Don turned to where he could hear the ladies' voices.

"She is? That makes it more difficult for her, doesn't it? She's met your parents?"

"She has. Last night. Aidan dropped us off there. Dad brought us home." Don rubbed at his face, not sure what to say. "She needs us, Mark, and I just don't know how to proceed."

Chapter 10

Don's team were on their feet as Don entered the conference room. Mark had headed out before Don, shaking his head at the team. They shared looks with one another before looking past Don to where Delanie was hesitating in the hallway. Don dropped his paperwork on the table and then left to stand in front of Delanie before he hugged her.

Turning back to the room, Don bit at his lip. This was a huge step for him and also for Delanie. He knew how the team would react. Delanie didn't. She had been thrown into something that she shouldn't have been. They had felt as if they had had no choice. He had prayed it through thoroughly before he asked her. Don knew that Delanie had been praying about that situation they were in. She had told him that.

The men were on their feet, smiles on their faces. They had often discussed who would be Don's bride and what she would look like. Delanie was the very picture of what they had imagined.

"Guys? This is Delanie. She is my bride. I know." Don's hand went up to stop the questions. "We'll discuss it. For now, we need to spend time in prayer and with your ladies. I know that they are here as well. Apparently from what McKala said, they know Delanie from church."

"They do, Don. I just didn't connect them with your team. I would have had no reason to. I had never met you before that day on the trail." Delanie was puzzled by that. "And I want to know why they went after you."

"So do we." Mark spoke for the group. "How be we spend that time in prayer that you wanted, Don? It's what we do, Delanie. We start our day off with prayer."

"And that has kept you safe over the years. We can do that. Then, I need to head for my office. I can only imagine the work waiting for me."

Taran wrapped an arm around Delanie, knowing that she felt very out of place right at that moment.

"We'll all go with you. We like to tag along on the adventures. And we will help you get caught up. It's what we do. We take care of one another."

An hour later, Don stood in the driveway watching as the ladies left. He had wrapped Delanie in a hug, dropped a kiss on her temple, and then sent her on her way. He sighed as he turned back to the office. This was where it became hard, Don knew, in trying to come to an understanding of what had happened.

Paul stared at Don for a moment before his eyes dropped to the papers in front of him. He had been investigating Delanie. He wasn't sure how much Don knew about his bride.

"It's okay, Paul. I know she from up north and is estranged from her family. She has often wondered if she was really theirs." Don reached for the papers, reading through them.

"I don't think that she is. Emma reached out when you were outside. She had Jace and Evan working on this for now. They'll forward what they find. They are of the same mind that she isn't."

"That may well be." Don stared across the room, uncertain as to what to say. Then, he just began to speak, telling them what had happened.

The men shared looks. They had a good idea just how Don was feeling at that point. It was always that way when an investigation started.

"Don, did you recognize the men?" Joshua looked around for a moment.

"No, I didn't. They just seemed to come out of the blue. And I was unconscious not long after they stuffed us into the van. Delanie has written out what she could." Don was puzzled. "We were locked into separate rooms. Then the next morning, she was able to leave her room and find me. The door locked after her. She did say that she could hear movement outside the door and what she described as a diabolical laugh."

The men froze. That sounded familiar somehow. They just had to think about it. It would come to them at some point.

Don was on his feet hours later. He was restless and worried about Delanie. He had no idea where her office was.

Caleb studied him, an amused look on his face. He approached Don and handed him a slip of paper.

"Here. This is where she is. Go and find her." He slapped Don on the back and walked into the office building again. They were not leaving yet. Caleb was thankful that they didn't have a team in that week for training. That meant that they could work on Don's adventure and maybe solve it quickly. He just didn't think that they would.

Delanie looked around her office that afternoon. With the ladies' help, she had been able to catch up on what she needed to do. She sighed to herself. It was to the point that she needed to hire a secretary. She just didn't want another person in the office.

Cullea looked up as Delanie walked into the kitchenette. She had been making coffee or tea for them all.

"Delanie? Where are you now with your work?"

"Thanks to you ladies, I am caught up. Having you take care of the paperwork was wonderful. I know that I need a secretary. I'm just not sure about bringing anyone in at present."

"That's understandable. How be we ladies decide who can be with you when you're here? Daci will want to be involved and so will Deree. You're family to us and we take care of our family." Cullea frowned as Delanie's face crumpled. "Delanie? What did I say?"

"That we're family. I never had that. And I don't know why. I used to ask why they hated me. They just shoved me aside." She looked up as she heard the other ladies in the room. "What family does that?"

"Maybe you aren't theirs? Don was muttering something about that." Payton reached to hug Delanie.

"And we are huggers, Delanie. Get used to that." She grinned at her.

"I am getting used to that. I never had many hugs in my life." She looked up as she heard a man's voice and was across the room and in Don's arms.

Chapter 11

A week later, Delanie ran for her car, fear driving her feet to race along the pavement. She could hear the pounding of the feet on the sidewalk behind her before she was tackled and taken down. Her face scraped along the sidewalk. Delanie cried out in pain and fear.

The man simply held her down, his eyes searching around them. No one seemed to be around and for that he was glad. He had been told to find this woman and threaten her. That he could do very well.

He shoved at her back and then rose, standing over her. An envelope was dropped in front of her before he ran for the shadows, leaving Delanie to lie still.

Delanie didn't rise for a few moments. She heard voices nearby and didn't respond, too afraid that the man had come back. Helped to a sitting position, Delanie looked around, a hand on her face.

Aidan had been driving by and saw the crumpled form on the sidewalk. He was out of the car and running towards the lady, he discovered. He was on his knees beside her, a dismayed look on his face. He had not expected to find Delanie.

Back at his car, Aidan called for help and then was back beside Delanie. He frowned as he saw the envelope lying in front of her. He reached for it with a gloved hand and then stood and watched as the paramedics worked on Delanie.

Toryn approached him, a frown on his own face.

—

"Delanie?"

Aidan nodded, his eyes on the horizon.

"I was driving by and found her. And this." He held up the envelope. "I haven't looked at it yet but I will. She hasn't roused since I found her."

"And we need to get Don to her." Toryn prayed for his friend and his bride. "This is getting bizarre, Aidan. Do you have any sense of why?"

Aidan shook his head. He didn't know why Don had been targeted. None of them did. There just wasn't enough to understand why.

"We just don't have enough to understand it. And there have been all those events hanging over from the others. Joshua and Jincy? We never did get a feeling on why they were forced to marry."

"No, we never did. There was always a feeling that something was left over." Toryn walked away, heading for a meeting that he had to be at. He was troubled for his friend and for his friend's bride.

Aidan walked towards Don as he stood near his office building. The others had already left for the day as had the team that was in for training. He prayed for his friend and his bride. This was not over, not by a long shot, and Aidan was afraid that one or the other would end up dead.

"Aidan? You're here? I wasn't expecting you." Don stared at him for a moment before his eyes closed. "Delanie?"

"Delanie. I was driving down a street and saw someone on the sidewalk. It was Delanie. She's at the hospital. Come on. I'll take you there." Aidan pointed at his car.

"Who did it?" Don fastened his seatbelt, his mind racing as to why and who.

"We don't know. I have officers trying to retrieve video footage. There was a letter near her."

"A letter? They threatened us, didn't they?" Don was positive that this is what happened.

"They did. It's vague enough though that we can't determine who it is. Just the usual of do what we say and we know where you live." Aidan pulled to a stop in the designated police parking spot at the hospital. His hand rested on Don's arm. "Before you go in, Don, let me pray with you."

Don nodded, knowing that his friends were praying for him but that he still needed to have that. His prayer was that God would defend his lady against whoever it was. And that was difficult to acknowledge that they had no idea who it was.

Don paced towards the examination room where Delanie was being assessed. He hesitated in the doorway, not seeing any hospital staff with her. Within seconds, he was across the room, her hand in his tight grasp. His other hand rested on her cheek, pain on his face as he saw the scrapings. Don bent over to drop a kiss on the cheek, finding that she turned towards him.

Dr. Bob Rogers walked into the room, reading Delanie's chart. He knew Delanie from church but by a different last name. He frowned as he looked up and found Don there.

"Don? Is she one of your protected persons?" Bob grinned at Don for a moment.

Don sighed. It had not gotten around that much that he and Delanie were married.

"It's a long story, Bob. Delanie and I are married. She's my bride." Don knew there would be no censure from Bob.

"She is? Off on one of those adventures that you young people seem to think that you need?" Bob didn't wait for Don to respond. "She's a fortunate young lady. She did manage to knock herself out but other than a headache and the scrapes on her face, physically she's fine. She's sleeping right now. We'll let you take her home soon." Bob watched Don carefully, seeing that Don was trying hard to cover up his worry. "Don? She's going to be fine. And so are you. I heard about your adventure a week or so ago. You are looking at trying to solve this but you both need time to heal and not just physically. Make sure that you both find someone to talk to."

"We have, Bob. Thanks for your concern." Don looked around for a chair and sat, his hand reaching for Delanie's again. He would wait until she was ready to go. Then he sighed. He didn't have a vehicle to take her home.

David appeared at his side, his hand on his son's shoulder. Aidan had reached out to him, just asking him to be with Don. Delanie had been hurt and Don needed his father.

—

Don looked up at his father. David drew in his breath at the devastation on his son's face.

"Son?"

"Delanie was attacked, Dad, and hurt. And I don't have my truck to take her home." Don was almost in tears, the stress of the last couple of weeks driving him to that as well as the worry about his bride.

"That's okay, son. I'll take you home. And I'll get Delanie's keys and have someone bring her car home if she can tell us where it is."

Don sighed, knowing that he didn't know. He reached for her purse, reluctant to look into it, but knowing that he had to. He found her keys and handed them to his father.

"She was at work, Dad, so it's likely there. She would have just been finishing work."

Chapter 12

Delanie rose before dawn the next morning. She was still terrified but determined to go on with her life. She hesitated outside Don's bedroom, assuming that he was still asleep. He had carried her into the house the night before and to her bedroom, watching as she sat on the side of the bed before he had hugged her and prayed for her before he walked away.

Standing on the back porch, Delanie studied the yard. She felt something off but was not familiar enough with it to know there really was. She would need to talk to Don about that. Delanie sipped at her tea before she sighed. She needed to be in the office that morning. Her face was aching as was her head and that would make it difficult.

Don was on his feet an hour later, searching for Delanie. She was not in the house. He began a systematic search and ended up in the driveway. Her car was gone. Don's head dropped. She had taken off and he didn't hear that. That was not good. He reached for his phone, dialling her number.

"Delanie? Are you okay? And just where are you?" Don's voice held a tone of panic.

Delanie roused from the grant paperwork that she had been immersed in. She searched for her phone, finding it buried under the paperwork. She frowned and then sighed. Delanie knew that she had meant to leave a note for Don and had forgotten. A simple text was shot off to him, letting him know that she was sorry and that she had meant to leave a message for him. She was fine and at the office.

Don drew in a sigh of relief. It was hard learning how to be part of a couple. His eyes raised to the sky. *Lord, I need Your help to do this. I want to protect and defend my bride but I just don't know how to. She's independent and I get that. I just worry when she's not with me. Thank You that You do defend us against evil.*

Late that afternoon, Don dropped down from Thomas's truck. Thomas had been more than willing to drop Don off at Delanie's office. It was Friday and they were done work for the weekend. They all had their plans and would meet again on Mon day.

Thomas watched Don carefully, seeing the stress that he was trying to hide.

"Stay safe this weekend, Don. No more adventures like a couple of weeks ago." Thomas grinned at his team leader.

"No, we don't want that again." Don looked around, seeing that Delanie's car was still there. "This is tough, you know."

"It is. You want to keep her safe and yet let her have her freedom. It's different for you. You're married to her and trying to work that out as well. Joshua and Jincy would know how you feel."

"They do and we've talked. Have a great weekend, Thomas. And thanks." Don walked into the office building, looking for his bride.

—

Delanie looked up, startled to hear footsteps heading her way. Her hands clenched until she recognized Don's voice.

"Don? What are you doing here?" Delanie was on her feet and in his arms.

"Looking for my bride." Don dropped a kiss on the scrape on her cheek. "And how is she feeling today?"

Delanie suddenly hugged him tighter, feeling cherished, loved, defended, and protected. Her heart was raised in thanks to God for who He had provided for her.

"I'm okay, Don. The scrape will heal. The headache is gone. And I've managed to get the grant applications done all ready. I usually take days to do that." Delanie looked at her desk. "The ladies' help the other day got me caught up. I had been struggling. I think that's why I took off that weekend. I needed to get away and clear my head."

Don began to laugh at that, knowing just how well that had gone over.

"No, that didn't work out so well. We know how well that went over." Don leaned against the door frame. "All ready to pack up for the weekend?"

Delanie stared at her desk. For the first Friday in months, she could leave the office and know that she didn't have anything waiting for her to rush through on Monday. She nodded, reaching to lock away what she needed to and then lock up her desk. Don reached for her hand and then led her to the entry door, watching as she set the alarm.

Standing beside her car, he reached for her keys. Delanie eyed the keys and then Don before she sighed. He was reaching out to take care of her and she wasn't used to that.

"I would like to take you out for dinner, sweetheart. Ben's diner is just down the street. Would that work?"

"It would. I go in there about once a week for a meal. He knows what I want before I can even ask."

"Ben does that." Don's hand reached for hers as they walked away from her car. "He can't explain how he does that."

Ben watched them as Don slid onto the seat beside Delanie. He frowned for a moment. He wasn't aware that either one was dating and certainly not one another. Ben walked over and just stood, waiting for them to look up.

"Don? Delanie? How are you two tonight?" Ben slid onto the seat across from them.

"We're just fine, Ben." Don grinned at him, knowing that Ben would not ask the question that he wanted to. "Just for your information, Delanie and I are off on an adventure. And we are married."

Ben nodded, his prayers raising for the couple. He knew that Don would face far worse than his team had.

"I wasn't aware that you two were dating but congratulations."

—

"It's a story, Ben. We were kidnapped and then we decided to marry." Don's arm wrapped around Delanie and pulled her closer to him.

"I see. Then you need our prayers. Your dinner will be out shortly." Ben rose, hesitated, and then walked away. He was greatly troubled by that news.

Don looked around, feeling someone watching him. He nodded at the people who he knew. There were a number of strangers in there and anyone could be the one watching them. He set it aside for the moment, content to out and about with Delanie and sharing a meal with her.

—

Chapter 13

Monday found Don settling behind his desk in his office. He could hear the voices of his team and smiled. At the moment, he was happy and content. Delanie had headed for her office not long before that. He worried about her travelling on her own but there was not a lot he could do about it. There was a team in for training and he had to be there.

Mark hesitated at Don's doorway, assessing him. He had been puzzling it all out over the weekend and had come to no clear conclusion.

"Don? Did anything happen over the weekend?" Mark sat in front of the desk, worried about his friend.

Don shook his head. He had been waiting for something to happen and nothing had. He had just felt watched wherever he and Delanie had been out around the town.

"No. And that has us puzzled. We know someone is following us and watching us. We just don't know who." Don sat back in his chair, his pen tapping on the table. "And we don't have enough information to figure this out."

"Has Emma come through with anything?"

"Not yet. She's been pulled into a number of urgent investigations. I told her that was okay and that we'd speak later this week. Now, about this team? What are your feelings?"

Mark nodded. They all had reservations about it.

"They should have been here by now and aren't. And I don't know that we've had any word from them."

Don was on his feet, finding his team heading his way.

"Guys?"

Thomas's face was grim. He held up evidence bags.

"Someone's been around here, Don. I can't get any clear image of who it was. But these were around the building. We'll need to do a better search of here, your home, and Delanie's office. What about her apartment?"

Don studied the cameras before he nodded.

"We cleared it out on the weekend and turned in the keys. She has good security on her building but we do need to go over it. Mark, you and Paul head that way. Joshua, Caleb, start the search around the house. Thomas, you and I are searching the training facility. This can't be allowed to continue." Don walked away, anger sparking from him before he prayed for his team and the facilities where they worked. Someone could set anything and they might not find it in time. That had almost happened to Mark when someone set a bomb under his bedroom.

Aidan turned as Mark approached him as he walked back towards the police department. He frowned. He thought that Mark would be deep in training that day.

"Mark?" Aidan stopped as Mark held up the bags he had taken from Thomas.

"This. We found them around the office building. We've just searched everywhere we can."

"They're starting that? Where's Don and Delanie?"

"Don's at the office trying to figure this out. Paul is with Delanie. He's not leaving her alone and she's protesting about that." Mark grinned for a moment as he recalled the fierce look on her face. "Don has his hands full with Delanie."

"That he will." Aidan grinned in return even as he reached for the bags. "They really wanted to watch you all."

"They do. And we couldn't get a clear look at who it was. And there was more than one person." Mark hesitated for a moment. "The team that was supposed to be in for training never showed and never called."

"They didn't? And I know your team. You would have investigated them prior to taking them on."

"We did. We're going back over it and don't see any red flags. But we're going to dig deeper. For now, we're searching even deeper into each team that is coming in." Mark waved as he walked away, leaving Aidan staring at the bags of cameras.

Delanie watched Paul as he paced her office. She had wanted to leave and he had refused to let her without saying why. That did not sit well with her.

She prayed about her attitude, knowing that the men were doing what they could to protect her.

"Paul? Why are we waiting?"

"This is the time that you usually leave, correct?"

"It is. Is that a problem?"

"There is. You need to vary the time that you come and go. If you keep to your schedule, then someone could be waiting for you to come or go." Paul gave a sad smile.

Delanie stared at him for a moment before she nodded. He was correct. She was a creature of habit when it came time for her to come and go.

"I guess I need to not do that." Delanie looked around her office. "I can work from home if I need to. That would probably be better."

"It might be. What do we need to pack up for you to do that?" Paul's hands were there to help.

Mark appeared as they worked away, helping to pack up her paperwork.

"What else, Delanie?" Mark came back in from packing the boxes into his truck.

"I think that's all for now." Delanie reached for her keys, finding Paul's hand there to take them from her. "Paul?"

"You ride with Mark. He'll follow me as I take your car back to your home."

Delanie stared at him, realizing that it was her home. Don had made her aware that it was. She sighed to herself. *Lord, how do I do this? I feel as if I have brought trouble to him. Or is it the other way around, Don has brought trouble to me? I know that You are here and present in the midst of this. You promise to never leave us or forsake us and to defend us. We just might not like the path that You have decided that we walk.*

Don turned from the stove where he was working on a meal for them. He heard the men's voices and then Delanie's. He shut off the stove burners and walked towards the office, nodding as Mark and Paul passed him. Don stood for a moment, watching Delanie as she worked away.

"Delanie?" His voice caused her hands to pause before she continued tidying away her work. "What's this?"

"Paul and Mark decided that I should not work in the office for now but from here. Not unless I have to. Even then, they tell me that someone will be with me." Delanie blinked back tears. This is not how she felt her day should end.

Don wrapped her into a hug, his chin resting on her head.

"It's tough, sweetheart, but probably for the best. We found cameras around the office building and that's why they headed in to search your building. If needed, we can set up an office for you in the building. And still get you to your office when you need to meet with anyone. Does that work?"

"It will for now. I hate this, Don. I really do."

"So do I. But if it wasn't for this, I would not have you in my life and as my bride. I would hate to think that you would not be here with me."

Chapter 14

Three days had passed since the men had found the cameras. A daily search had not found anything else. That day, Joshua stared at the vehicles and then searched, finding tracking devices on them. That had happened overnight. He sighed as he walked back into the office and to the security room.

Don found Joshua copying portions of the video feed and questioned him.

"There were tracking devices on the vehicles. They were in again overnight, whoever it was coming in to do it early this morning. Once more, we can't get any clear images of whoever it was."

Don sighed. This was just going to continue, wasn't it?

"Get them to Aidan, Joshua. And take the video clip with you." Don walked away, his shoulders slumping for a moment. This was not going anywhere.

Delanie saw Don walking towards her and just reached to hug him. They were talking about where they wanted to go with their marriage and were getting closer. Neither wanted to be apart from each other but then neither wanted to bring any danger to one another.

"Don?"

"Delanie? You were looking for me?" Don reached to kiss her cheek.

"I was. Joshua was around the vehicles. What did he find?"

"Tracking devices. And whoever it is will be back at some point. They're quite bold."

"They are and they will continue to do this. It's a game with them." Delanie was well aware of what to expect. "How do we do this, Don?"

"We continue to live our lives. We go out on dates, go for walks, visit my family. Daci has asked if we could come for a meal tonight. I said I'd ask."

Delanie had grown to love Daci. She was the sister that she had never had.

"I would like that. You need to be with your family. Daci isn't around her like she used to be, is she?" Delanie grinned at Don.

"No, she's not and I miss that. She's been a good companion over the years. I'm sorry that you didn't have that." Don hugged her. "Now, let's get through our day and then we can enjoy our time tonight." He walked away, leaving her frowning after him.

Payton and Cullea shared a grin before they moved in on Delanie.

"Delanie?" Payton's voice startled Delanie.

"Payton? Cullea? You're here?" Delanie reached to hug the ladies.

"We're here to help you and to work in Don's office. We do that. Now, what are we up to for you?" Cullea grinned as well before she headed to the office that Delanie was using.

"I have no idea. I'm caught up, thanks to you all. I just need to go through what I have coming up and that doesn't usually take long. Then I return some phone calls." Delanie paused for a moment, a thought niggling at her. "What if it's someone who I refused to help?"

"That's always possible." Payton moved past her, heading for the front office. "And you can't share with anyone because of your confidentiality contract."

"No, I can't. I have to go through them all on my own, I guess. I don't remember anyone who stood out. They are usually grateful for whatever help that I can give them. If I can't help too much, they understand. I work with those who have limited funds." Delanie chewed at her bottom lip, suddenly unsure of what she was doing. Had she brought this on herself? She prayed that she had not.

Cullea hugged her and then turned her into the office that she was using. Delanie moved to sit behind the desk, watching as Cullea found a seat in front of it.

"How do I know?" Delanie was almost in a panic, thinking that she had brought this on them.

"You not likely will. Go through your clients and see if anything stands out. You can always take your concerns to Aidan." Cullea stared at her friend. "We need to make this a matter of prayer."

"We do. Don and I have been but it just doesn't seem to be resolving." Delanie propped her chin on her hand. "How do we do this?"

"We keep working on it. Keep a journal, Delanie. Write down anything that comes to you."

Delanie nodded, knowing that Cullea was correct. She looked around as she heard footsteps. Caleb appeared in the doorway before he entered to perch on the arm of his wife's chair.

"Delanie? What can we do for you?" He grinned as she snorted.

"Solve this. I understand that this has been going on for months. It's wearing all of you out, particularly Don. How do we do this?"

Caleb nodded. Don had been adamant that Delanie would want to work on solving their adventure and that one of the men needed to talk with her.

"What can you tell us, Delanie?" Caleb moved to sit, reaching for a pad of paper and pen. "Talk to us. We know that you're not from this town. Tell us when you moved here, about your home life when young, about your parents."

Delanie glared at him, hearing Cullea laughing.

"In other words, you want to pick my brain." She continued glaring at Caleb as he began to laugh as well.

"Delanie, you are so good for this group." Caleb grinned wider as she snorted. "You are. You are exactly who Don needs."

"Yeah, well about that. We didn't think that we had much choice." Delanie's face grew sad.

Caleb sobered, hearing Cullea muttering something under her breath.

—

"Don would not have asked you to marry him, Delanie, if he had not prayed through it and felt that God had given him permission to go ahead with it. That's the character of your groom. We are all like that. Joshua and Jincy didn't have a choice. They were forced to marry. You and Don did. You could have walked away from him and left. He would have watched out for you from a distance. That's what he does."

Delanie had watched Caleb soberly, not seeing that Don was hesitating just outside the door. She thought through what had been said and nodded. That was true, she acknowledged to herself. Don had been hesitant to ask her. She could tell that from how he had asked her.

"I get that, Caleb. We just need to work through some things." Delanie looked up at that point, seeing Don watching her. She frowned slightly at the look on his face, a look that said that he cherished and loved her and would do anything he could to defend and protect her.

Chapter 15

Don turned late that afternoon, hearing Aidan's voice. He offered a quick prayer that Aidan was there to tell them that it was all over. He didn't think that was why he was there.

"Aidan?" Don stood in his kitchen doorway, watching as Aidan walked towards him. Delanie gave him a glance and then walked away. He sighed. He needed her there to hear what Aidan had to say.

"I'm here as a friend, Don. Nothing more. I'm off duty tonight. It's been a while since we did that. Where did Delanie go to?" Aidan looked around, surprised to find that she had disappeared.

"Likely to the office. She's been working through some things and I've just let her be. Let me find her." Don went to walk around Aidan when that man laid his hand on Don's arm stopping him. "Aidan?"

"Let her be for now. I'll talk with her later. But you? How are you actually doing? I ran into Gideon this afternoon. He's wanting to talk to both of you but has that conference this weekend."

Don sighed, knowing that he did indeed need to speak with their pastor. He had been avoiding that and just why that was, he couldn't say.

"Yeah, we do need to do that. I'll call him next week or catch him on Sunday." Don stared ahead of himself, not seeing the framed fall photo on the wall in front of him. "This has been unfair to Delanie."

———

"And to you. You didn't think that you had any other choice. And we all know that you would have prayed this through."

"I did. It's still not right. She's a beautiful and compassionate lady. She should have been courted and allowed to make her own choice of who she married." Don didn't see Delanie standing nearby.

Aidan did and saw the look on her face. He nodded. These two were falling in love with one another right in front of their eyes. That was what had happened with the others.

"Don? Delanie could have said no. She didn't. God was there in the midst of all of it. This is one way that He chose to defend and protect you both. We still don't have a line of who or why. But for now, let's set this aside and just spend time together as friends." He looked at Delanie again, seeing her nodding before she moved to hug Don and then hug Aidan.

Delanie whispered a soft thank you to Aidan before she walked past him into the kitchen. Don had been working on a salad and she just took up that task. Aidan walked past her to the back door and the grill, knowing Don likely had something on the grill. And he was correct. The chicken was almost ready, he noted.

Don turned to watch Delanie, realizing that she had heard his words. He stopped beside her, an arm around her. His mouth opened and closed before he spoke. And he just wasn't sure what to say.

Delanie shot him a glance and then nodded. He wasn't sure what to say, was he?

"It's okay, Don. We agreed to marry. God was there as Aidan has said. He would have stopped us if it was not His will for us. We forget that He is in control."

"And you are right. He is in control. Thank you for being who you are, Delanie. You are a courageous companion in all this. I have no idea how much danger that we will face. I would not want to walk through it with anyone else but you." Don's kiss dropped on her forehead and then he walked outside to find Aidan removing the meat from the grill.

The next morning, Don faced Delanie across the kitchen table. His hands rested on the back of a chair while she had her arms wrapped around herself. She was shaking her head, not willing to do what he had asked of her.

"We need to be out and about, sweetheart. This won't get resolved if we continue to hide. All I am asking is that we go out to Ben's for lunch." Don walked around the table and simply hugged her.

"I know, Don. I'm just so afraid today. And I know that God is protecting us. It's just that I am so afraid."

"I know that, Delanie. So am I. But I am making the choice that fear is not going to rule my life. I would like that for you too. I understand that it is hard."

"It is. I think that I have been afraid all of my life."

Don stared at her and then made a decision.

"Come on, sweetheart. Let's get changed and head to Elmton for the day. A good friend of mine lives there and he can help try and sort through this." He sent off a quick text to Richard and received confirmation that Richard would be home that day. "He's home. We walk back and forth in each other's lives. He has a security team and they all went through some stuff."

"What is it with your friends?" Delanie walked away, happiness suddenly in her heart. Don had not shoved aside her concerns but had validated them and tried to find a way to help her.

Richard stood and watched as Don pulled into his driveway. He saw Don drop from the truck and move around to help Delanie down. He nodded as he wrapped an arm around his wife, Raleigh.

"That's Delanie? She looks familiar." Raleigh walked towards the other couple to hug Don and then Delanie. "Hi, Delanie. I'm Raleigh, Richard's wife. I am so glad to meet you." Raleigh kept her arm around Delanie as she moved them towards the house.

Richard waited for Don to approach him, studying his friend. Don was bearing a heavy burden and had been for a while, given what his team had been through.

"Don? Want to talk?"

Don nodded, knowing that his life-long friend would be a good one to be a sounding board.

"I do. But for now, let's find our ladies."

Richard grinned at him as Don said that.

<hr>

“It sounds strange to hear you refer to your lady. But she seems to be just who you need.”

“She is. And I am afraid that when this is all over, she’ll walk away on me.” Don grew sad at that thought, his heart hurting at that.

Chapter 16

Delanie was on her feet early the next morning. She stared at Don's closed bedroom door as she walked by it before she headed for the living room and her Bible. Staring across the room before she started a search, Delanie made a decision. She was not going to sit back any more. She was planning on going on the offensive.

Don rose later, a frown on his face as he stared at the clock. It was too late not to make it to church. He sighed. He really needed to be there that day. Walking through the house, Don paused in the living room. He could see that Delanie had been there but wasn't. He sighed. He needed to find her, he decided.

Stopping in the kitchen, he poured himself a mug of coffee and then headed for the back porch. He smiled as he saw Delanie curled up on the swing before he joined her, an arm around her to draw her to him.

"Morning, sweetheart." Don dropped a kiss on her temple.

"Good morning, Don. You slept in."

"I did. We won't get to church this morning." Don was disappointed at that.

"No, we won't but they have a live stream that we can catch later. You must have needed that sleep."

"I guess." Don grew quiet, content to sit there in silence.

"Don? Where do we go from here to find whoever it is? We can't continue as we are." Delanie spoke at last, hating to break the silence.

"I don't know, sweetheart. We're working on it. Aidan is and so are Emma and her group. Whoever this is? They've hidden themselves well. We're not getting everything that usually appears."

"We're not. Does that mean that they are really close to us? Among our friends?" Delanie was afraid of that. She just didn't want to verbalize it.

"It's possible. It wouldn't be the first time that something like that happens." Don shifted his seat, drawing her closer to him, desperate to protect and defend the love of his life.

"Then, we list who we know, their relatives, friends, and work out from there." Delanie shifted as well to stare up at him. "Is that what we do?"

"It is. It is difficult for us as we both have had clients who may wish us harm. We need to look through those as well. And that will be difficult. They could have hidden themselves well."

Delanie sighed. Don was correct. It would be difficult but it was so necessary. Don's arm tightened around her. He was afraid for both of them but particularly for Delanie. When she was out and about, she was on her own.

"We'll look into your family as well, sweetheart. We've talked about maybe you are not their biological child. What more thoughts do you have on that?"

—

Delanie nodded. That had been her thought as well. She turned back to Don, a thought crossing her mind.

"If they're not, then who are my parents and where are they?"

Don sighed. She had gone to the heart of the matter.

"Emma is looking into that for us. She thought that she might have information tomorrow. We'll go over it together. Emma never provides any information that she has not proven. That's how she is."

"That's good, I guess." Delanie grew pensive before she stared at the back of the yard. "Don? What's back there? Something is that wasn't there yesterday."

Don followed where her shaking finger had pointed and nodded. He was on his feet, pulling her into the house and locking the door behind them. His phone was out to call in the authorities. He would not go near it. Delanie needed him with her.

George walked back towards the house. Delanie had good eyes, he decided. That bundle contained a bomb, set to go off at noon.

"George?" Don unlocked the back door and opened it, letting George into the kitchen.

"Don? There was a bomb back there, set to go off at noon. Delanie has good eyes."

"She does." Don turned to find Delanie nearby. "What can you tell us about it?"

"Not a lot. We need to take a good look at it and then at your security feed."

"We've searched it. Nothing shows up. It was too dark." Don was frustrated at that. "They've brought it to our home, George. How do we stay safe?" Don's hand waved in the air. "I know. I know. I know how to do that. It's different when it's personal."

"It is. And we can't tell you how to stay safe. You need to make those decisions yourself. It may come to a point where we tuck you away somewhere. You know how that works." George spoke with them for a while longer and then left, disturbed that another friend had been threatened like that.

Don nodded. He knew only too well how that worked and how the people who were tucked away felt. He had done that as a security team for far too many people. Don reached for Delanie, wrapping her tight to him. Her arms were around him even as she was shaking with fear. This bomb? It had scared both of them.

George stayed for a while, sharing a meal with them before he was off to another crime scene. He was deeply worried about Don and planned to speak with whoever it was that he needed to. And those people included Don's team.

Late that night, Don paused beside Delanie as she slept, curled up in a corner of the couch. He had a soft smile before he was beside her and turned her to sleep against his shoulder. Reaching for a blanket, he spread it out over them and then slept himself. He

———

didn't feel the little calico cat as she crept up and cuddled up close to their faces. She slept as well after a little pink tongue had come out to wash a little white foot.

None of them roused as activity was heard outside of the house. If they had, they perhaps would have thought that it was just the wind. Only there was no wind that night. The men who were working away kept their heads down and their faces hidden. One of them had taken the time to cover the cameras for the time that they were working there.

Chapter 17

Don roused the next morning as he heard the doorbell. He looked around, rubbing at his eyes, surprised to find himself in the living room. The little cat stretched, disturbed at him for making her move. He stared down at Delanie before he rose and headed for the door, rubbing at his head.

Thomas and Mark stood there, the other three having headed for the office building. They were disturbed, to say the least, at what they saw around the house.

"Don? We woke you up." Thomas was surprised at that.

"You did. Come in and I'll put on the coffee while I change."

Thomas's hand stopped him from moving backwards into the house. Instead, he pulled Don outside.

"Did you hear anything last night?" Mark's voice was harsh.

"No. I didn't. Why?" Don stared at Mark and saw the anger in his friend. "Mark?"

"Walk around your house, Don. See what happened overnight. Joshua is heading for the security feed to see what he can find out."

Don stared at Mark in shock and then at Thomas before he was out of the house and walking around it. He stared in shock and then horror at the mock gravestones that were placed at fifteen-foot intervals. Don didn't need to read them to know that they were directed at both himself and Delanie. That disturbed him greatly.

"How did they manage to do this?" Don stared at the last one, one reading his own name. There was no date of death but he clearly read the threat.

"That we don't know." Joshua had walked over to them. "The security cameras had something over them for however long it took to do this. The group managed to sneak in undercover and do that. They are very familiar with our property."

Don nodded, having come to that conclusion.

"We go back through all the teams that have been through here. We get the names to Emma and have her and her team investigate them. It comes back to one of them or someone close to them."

"That it does, Don. And somehow, Delanie is involved. We think it's just because she was there but there may be something that does connect you two." Thomas was adamant about that.

"I know, Thomas. How far have we gotten on our own investigation?" Don walked back around the house and into it, his team following him. He searched for Delanie and heard the shower running.

Thomas walked back out of the house and then pulled out his phone. Aidan was not surprised to hear from him. He was just surprised to hear what they had found.

—

Ten minutes later, Delanie stood outside the house, staring at one of the gravestones. Her arms were wrapped around herself. Caleb and Paul stood on either side of her, their backs to her as they searched the area around her.

"Who did this?" Delanie's voice was harsh with her fear. Her prayers didn't seem to be calming her at all.

"We don't know, Delanie. They covered the cameras while they were working and then pulled them off as they left. We didn't get any images of them. I wish that we had and that we could end it right now." Paul was angry, more angry than he had ever been. He felt justified, even though he knew that he had to give his anger to God.

"They're starting to ramp it up, aren't they?" Delanie was resigned to that, knowing full well that would continue to build up.

"They are and this is when it does get more dangerous for both of you. Don is well aware of how this works. How do we protect you though, Delanie? You can't be caged." Paul was working through scenarios in his mind.

"You can't. You have a life outside of work. You are here training. I have to be out and about and that sometimes means I have to do that on my own. I have to be in the office in town at least three days a week now, given the meetings that I need to have." Delanie paused and then walked away, heading for the house. Retrieving her purse, she headed for her car and

———

then her office. She didn't see the car trailing after her. It wouldn't have made any difference if she had.

Delanie paced her office late that afternoon. She had met with a number of clients that day, trying her best to concentrate and not quite able to. She sighed to herself. Delanie secured her office and then headed for Ben's diner. She needed a break from everything and wasn't sure that she could get that.

Ben watched Delanie as she hesitated in the doorway before he beckoned to her and then sent her down the hall to his office. She sank into a chair, grateful for Ben's friendship. She knew from Payton that Ben and his wife had taken in Paul when Paul was forced to live on the streets. That didn't surprise her.

Appearing in his office, Ben set a tray down beside Delanie before he chose a chair beside her. Delanie was thankful for the mug of tea and the plate of toast. She had not eaten lunch and knew that had been a mistake.

"Delanie? Talk to me." Ben waited patiently for her to respond.

"Ben? What can I say? I'm in danger and I don't know who from. How do I find out?" She blinked rapidly, trying to control the tears that threatened to overflow.

"Don and his team are working on it, are they not? And so are friends of theirs." Ben prayed for his young friend.

"They are. It just isn't getting solved. And I am afraid that Don will be hurt or killed. That's what

—

they're threatening us with." Delanie continued to try and control her tears.

"They do that, Delanie. They are trying to frighten you enough that you run from protection or those who will defend you or that you make a mistake and they take you once more." Ben wasn't sure what else to say.

Delanie nodded, knowing that Ben was correct. She had to stay with Don or his men but she had to live her life as well. She just wasn't sure how to do that without bringing danger to someone.

Chapter 18

Don was waiting for Delanie that afternoon, puzzled that she had not yet arrived home. He reached for his phone, searching for any messages from her and not finding one. He was worried, to say the least. She was late and it was not her not to call or text him.

Delanie pulled into the parking spot that she used at home and watched as Don almost ran towards her. She opened her car door, a frown on her face before she was out of it and into Don's arms. He just held her as tightly as he could.

"I was worried, sweetheart." He loosened his hug enough to look down at her.

"I'm sorry. I stopped in at Ben's and we were talking. I didn't realize that time had gotten away. He walked me back to my car and looked it over for me." She grinned suddenly. "He's been around you guys too much."

Don laughed at that, knowing that Ben cared about his friends and would do what he could to protect them.

"He has been. Paul has been teaching him what to watch out for." Don wrapped an arm around her, taking her briefcase from her after she had locked up her car.

"Paul would do that, wouldn't he?" Delanie stood in the home office, frowning at the book shelves.

—

"It's not the book shelves' fault, Delanie." Don grinned at her once more. "Come on. I'm starved. And it is past suppertime."

"I'm sorry. Ben gave me tea and toast when I was there. I shouldn't have eaten." Delanie looked distraught.

Don walked back to her and stood with his hands on her arms.

"It doesn't matter, Delanie. If you don't want much, that's fine with me. Ben gave you what you needed at that point. I can grill some chicken and do a tossed salad. I'm not really all that hungry."

"No, I don't think any of us are. That sounds good." Delanie walked away to change into more casual clothing, leaving Don shaking his head before he headed for the kitchen.

Don paused as he stepped out of the back door and headed for the grill. His hand rested on it for a moment before he backed away from it. He ran back into the house, shouting for Delanie. She appeared in the hallway, the little calico cat in her arms. Don reached for her hand and snagged her purse at the same time, running from the house with her and as far from it as he could. The sudden unexpected explosion sent them flying to the ground, Don's body covering Delanie as debris scattered through the air.

Turning slightly, he stared back at his home, shock on his face. It was destroyed. Delanie sat up, cradling the little cat in her arms as tightly as she could, shock on her face.

"Don? The house?"

Don reached to hug her, holding on tightly despite the protests of the cat. It had been too close, he knew. His home was destroyed and that saddened him. A house could be replaced. Delanie could not.

"I know, Delanie. Thank God you're safe." His hug tightened before he had his phone out and was calling it in.

Don's team milled around at the foot of the driveway, shock on their faces. They were not allowed closer. Emergency vehicles crowded the driveway as the firefighters worked to contain the blaze and extinguish it. They could see Don and Delanie speaking with an officer before they headed towards the team.

Don hesitated as he saw the men before he ducked under the police line, drawing Delanie with him. He shook his head at them, pointing instead to Thomas's truck.

They headed for Thomas' house, Delanie sitting tight to Don. She refused to let go of the calico cat. She seemed to be Delanie's safety line to sanity. Taran stared at Don and then Delanie before she drew Delanie into the kitchen and shoved her into a chair. She paused as she saw the cat and turned to Thomas. Thomas nodded and was out of the house, heading for a store to buy supplies for the pet.

Don paced the living room, disturbed and scared. This had been too close, he knew. He also knew that his team wanted answers, answers that he didn't have.

—

He could hear the other wives as they arrived and headed for Delanie.

The remaining team members watched Don closely. All they knew is that Don's house was destroyed.

"Don? What happened?" Mark spoke for the men.

"A bomb, I think. I went out to grill chicken and couldn't open the grill. I grabbed for Delanie and ran. We just made it far enough away not to be hurt." Don was angry and also saddened. "Delanie was holding the calico and just didn't let go of her."

"Wow!" Paul spoke for the team. "In the grill?"

"We think so but until the investigation is complete, we won't know."

"And you have to find somewhere to stay." Caleb spoke up at that point. "You won't stay with your parents or Daci."

"After this? Not a chance. We can stay in the office building for now, I think, until we find something."

"No, you won't." Joshua pointed at Don. "There's a house right next to you that is for rent. Toryn owns it and it is up to date for security". Joshua walked away, his phone out to contact Toryn. He knew that Toryn would not hesitate to agree.

Toryn stood for a moment and studied Don and then Delanie. He had been shocked when George had tracked him down and told him what had happened. He had also been very agreeable to Joshua's request.

—

Don took the keys offered to him, shaking his head at Toryn. He had no idea who had done this but he wanted them and wanted them badly. They had almost killed the love of his life and that was not acceptable. He sighed and then surrendered them to the Lord. God had to be the Avenger for this, not him.

Chapter 19

Delanie paused as she reached for some sweaters in a store in town. She hated the fact that she had to replace everything and that Don had to as well. Don was beside her, worrying that Delanie was not talking much. He needed her to and she just wasn't obliging him.

"Delanie? We don't have to replace everything today. Just get what we really need." Don stopped her with an arm around her.

Nodding, Delanie stared at the clothes in the shopping cart.

"We shouldn't have to be doing this, Don. Who did this to us?" She blinked to control her tears. She also knew that Deree and Daci were around, trying to help. Delanie appreciated that more than she could say.

"I know that we shouldn't. And I have no idea who did this. I want them for this but also for threatening you. We could have been killed." Don paused his words, not sure how to continue. "You do realize that if you had been home in time, we could well have still been inside the house, cooking something in the kitchen."

Delanie turned her head, staring at Don in shock. She had not thought of that.

"So, what you're saying is that God delayed me by having me go to the diner and that saved our lives?"

She paled and swayed on her feet, Don's arm keeping her upright. "Don?"

"I know, sweetheart. I know. We could be in heaven right now but we're not. Here, let's pay for this and then head for Dad's. We can stay there tonight if you wish." Don waited for her to speak. "Toryn and our friends have moved in some furniture, enough for now."

"Can we go to the house, Don? Toryn did let you have the keys, didn't he?"

"He did. Toryn and our friends have moved in some furniture, enough for now. We'll stop and grab enough food to get us through to tomorrow. Come on, sweetheart. Let's head out." Don stopped by his mother and Daci who both nodded at his words.

Delanie woke in the night, shaking in fear. She was on her feet, trying the doors and windows before she headed for Don. She stared down at Don before she simply slid under the covers and cuddled up tight to him. Delanie needed that contact to feel safe.

Don roused somewhat and then just wrapped an arm around Delanie before he slept again. He too was afraid, more afraid than he had ever been in his life.

On her feet in the early morning, Delanie avoided Don for a while. She was embarrassed that she had been so afraid the night before. She headed for a shower and then stood staring at the new clothes. Tears clouded her vision for a moment. This was not how they had planned their Saturday.

Don was on his feet as well, roaming outside the house and then coming back inside. He found Delanie in the kitchen, making a simply meal for them. Don wrapped her into a hug, simply holding her as she wept. His own tears wet her hair.

"Don? What do we do today?" Delanie stepped away from him, reaching for the meal to set it on the table.

Don shrugged. He wasn't sure what they were to do. He had had a call from Aidan when he had been outside. They could not access his home area that day but likely would on the next day. Don needed to be in the office on Monday, to prepare for the team coming in for three days of training on Tuesday. He just wasn't sure that he would be able to.

"We have to speak with the insurance investigator and then we need to start making a list of what we need to purchase. I know, sweetheart. I know. We shouldn't have to do that but we do. Aidan will be around at some point." Don reached for her hand as they sat to eat their breakfast and asked a blessing on the meal.

Delanie kept shooting Don looks over the meal. She was not sure why he kept calling her sweetheart. He had her heart, she knew. She had fallen in love with her groom but didn't know if he loved her in return.

"Don? Why do you call me sweetheart?" Delanie finally grasped her fear of asking Don what he meant and through it away.

"Delanie? Why do I call you sweetheart?" Don reached for her hands. "It's because that's who you are.

You are my sweetheart. You're the one that I've been waiting for and prayed for. God brought us together and has kept us together and safe. I love you, Delanie. You are the missing part of me." Don watched with compassion and slight worry as her face crumpled. "Delanie?"

"Don? You mean that?" Delanie swiped at her face. Her emotions were raw from what they had been undergoing. She had not expected him to say that.

"I do, sweetheart. I don't know if you will ever love me in return. I will never walk away from you." Don reached to wrap her into his arms.

Delanie hugged him tighter than she ever had. She had come home, she decided, and thanked God for the man who He had allowed into her life.

"I love you, Don. I just didn't think that you would love me."

Don's hand slowed from where it had been rubbing at her back. He set her back slightly and then reached to kiss her. They would talk more, he knew, but for now he was content to hold the lady who he loved and who love him in return.

"We'll talk, sweetheart. We'll talk it out. For now, let's spend time in prayer. We need to replace our Bibles." He was saddened at that.

"We do." Delanie was on her feet, clearing away the meal and then heading with Don for the living room. She cuddled up tight to him, his arm around her. The little calico cat just jumped up on Delanie and curled up, her purr sounding in the air.

Don stood at the police tape that blocked his driveway. Delanie stood tight to him. The insurance investigator was there and walked towards them.

"Don? This is not what I expected to have to do for you." Bob Jones shook Don's hand and then turned to Delanie. "And this is your wife?"

"She is, Bob. This is Delanie. Now, what can you tell us?" Don ducked under the tape, pulling Delanie with him.

"It was a bomb as you suspected. God protected you last night." Bob went through the technical aspects of what he had found. "We know it wasn't you. You're too careful."

"Do you know if it was set in the grill?" Delanie stared at the debris that had been her home.

"No, actually it wasn't. It was set off to one side. You sensed something, Don, and that sent you running from the house."

"I did. I don't know that I really saw anything. My instincts kicked in and I reacted just as I would when we were out on an assignment."

"And that saved your lives." Bob spoke with the couple for a while longer before they all walked back to their vehicles.

Shutting the door after himself, Don reached for Delanie's hand. He prayed for them as a couple and then for safety. This was beginning to heat up and he was afraid for Delanie.

———

Chapter 20

Don paced outside of his office building on the Monday, his eyes on the debris from his home. It had devastated him when he saw that it had been destroyed. He wasn't sure who had been the mastermind behind it but someone was. Someone had a hate of for him and he wanted to know who.

The five members of his team stood around him, watching him and then studying the debris as well. The yellow caution tape around the site waved slightly in the breeze. They were all puzzled about it. None of them had expected Don and Delanie to have had that close of a call.

"Don? Where do you stand with all this?" Paul spoke for the team.

Don shrugged, turning to face them.

"I have no idea. This was not how we planned our weekend. I just thank God that we weren't hurt." Don rubbed at his face. He was exhausted and worried about Delanie. "Delanie is in her office in town. We have the team in tomorrow."

"We do. And all of us are needed for the training. We'll work it through. And we are working on this for you." Joshua walked into the building and to his desk. He sat, puzzled by it all. Caleb dropped into a seat in front of his desk.

"Joshua? What's your take on this?"

Joshua shrugged. Like the others, he had no idea what to think.

"I don't know what to think, Caleb. This is ugly." Joshua sat back in his chair. "How do we keep them safe?"

"That's going to be the problem, isn't it?" Caleb was on his feet, heading for the conference room.

Joshua watched and then followed him. He wasn't sure what Caleb was up to.

Caleb paced along the wall, studying what they had been able to find. It was not a lot, he decided, and knew that they would never solve it at this rate. Now, how could they move it along? He prayed for his friends, knowing that would be the only thing that would get Don and Delanie through all this.

Mark stood beside Joshua, a frown on his face. This was puzzling to them all and not one of them knew how to proceed. They had reached out to Emma and she was working it as well. She just wasn't finding what she thought that she should be.

Don approached his team, a frown on his face. The team that was due in for training was there as well. He sighed. He really didn't want to be there. Don wanted to be where Delanie was and couldn't.

Delanie walked back into her office building. She had been over to the courthouse and then the post office. She had felt followed but had not seen anyone who stood out to her. Delanie sorted through her mail, stopping at the plain white envelope. There was no name on it or an address and no return address. She dropped it back to the desk and backed away. She could feel the evil coming from it.

Aidan watched Delanie before he was past her and staring down at her desk. He snapped on gloves and reached for the envelope. Her call had come in just a few moments previously. He could hear the fear in her voice.

"You just got this?"

"I did. It was in with the mail that I just picked up at the post office. How did that get in there?" Delanie pointed a shaking finger at it.

"It was in the mail?" Aidan frowned at that. It shouldn't have happened. That meant someone in the post office was involved or had been asked to do that. This meant another level of investigation that he had not expected.

Aidan took photos of the envelope before he opened it. He pulled out the letter and frowned. The page was blank. This was not what he had expected.

"Aidan? What does it say?" Delanie moved forward to stand near him. "Aidan?"

"It's blank, Delanie."

"Blank? Why? That can't be!" Delanie's voice had her shock at his words.

"It is blank, Delanie." Aidan stared at the paper and then at her. He slipped the paper and the envelope into evidence bag and labeled them. "I'll take them to the lab and see what they can find for us."

"I don't get why. I felt followed today but didn't see anyone." Delanie sighed. She was exhausted from everything. She wanted her old life back but that would never happen. Don's declaration of his love for her had changed that. Delanie knew that he would defend her to his death if that's what was necessary.

Don walked through the house late that afternoon. The day had been frustrating to say the least. The team that was in for training was obstinate in not wanting to learn. Don's team had looked at one another and then met after the team had left. Don had called the team leader into his office and bluntly told him that if his team wasn't willing to learn then they needed to leave. The team leader had glared at Don and then walked away. Don was not sure that the team would be there the next day.

He looked for Delanie, not finding her at first. He stood in the bedroom doorway, finding her curled up on the bed, a blanket covering her. The little calico cat was curled on near her face, raising her head to stare at Don.

Don was on his knees beside the bed, an arm around his bride. He could see the traces of tears on her face and it broke his heart. He wanted whoever it was that was causing this. The team had talked that afternoon. They weren't sure if someone was only after Don or was after Delanie or after both of them. They just couldn't put a finger on it.

Don rose and reached for his comfort clothes. Showered and shaved, he dressed, pulling on black socks as he sat on the edge of the bed. His eyes went to Delanie. He would not waken her. She needed that sleep.

Delanie woke an hour later, feeling Don in the house. She rose and folded the blanket, a soft smile on her face as she touched her cheek. She knew that Don had dropped a kiss there. She had felt it in her sleep. Gathering the cat in her arms, Delanie walked through the house, studying it. It wasn't home, she decided. It never would be. She walked into Don's hug, knowing that he had been on guard, ready to defend her. Only, God was the One who would do that best, she knew. She could only pray for that and claim the promises that He gave in His Word.

Chapter 21

Don ran through the pouring rain on Saturday, heading for a shop in the nearby town of Riverville. He shook off as many of the raindrops as he could. He reached for Delanie's hand as he opened the door. She had stared at him that morning, not sure why he was asking what he was. She shook her head at him.

"Why this store, Don?" Delanie looked around with interest. It was one shop that she had avoided, not interested in trinkets and knick knacks.

"Just because. It's owned by a friend." Don grinned at her as he led her towards the employees only door at the back. He tapped and then peeked into the office. "Darcy?"

"Don? You're here?" Darcy was on her feet and greeting Don with a hug. She looked past him at Delanie who stood there, somewhat uncomfortable. "And who is this?"

"This is Delanie, my bride. A long story, Darcy. Just like our friends." Don watched as Darcy studied Delanie and then just hugged her.

"Welcome, Delanie. Here, come on in." Darcy watched as Delanie hesitated. "Or if you'd rather, we can wander the shop. I have items from many artists and am always looking for new artists to add to the shop."

Darcy moved away with Delanie, leaving Don to stand and watch the ladies. A soft smile covered his face. Darcy was being Darcy, reaching out to draw from the depths of Delanie to find out about her and then to decide how to help her. He didn't turn as he heard footsteps beside him.

Doug Foster watched Don and then Darcy, a frown momentarily covering his face for a few seconds. He then turned to Don, seeing the stress on his face.

"Don?"

Doug's voice reached through Don's dark thoughts. Don looked around and smiled at his friend.

"Doug? You're not on duty today?"

"Not today." Doug was the lieutenant in charge of Riverville's Emergency Task Force.

"That's good.   Is Darcy working all day? Delanie and I would really appreciate talking with you."

"Delanie? Who is she?"

"My bride.   It's a long story, Doug, but I welcome your thoughts. Is Abe around this weekend?"

"He is. We're due to have lunch with him and Emma. Introduce me to your wife."

Don wrapped an arm around Delanie, causing her to look up at him for a moment. He grinned at her.

"Find something, sweetheart?"

She nodded, happiness on her face for the moment. She held up a glass blown angel.

"This. I love angels. This is just so beautiful."

Don took it gently from her and examined it before he handed it to Darcy.

"Then, you shall have it." Don pointed at Doug. "This is Darcy's husband, Doug. They're having lunch with Emma and Abe. I just invited us to that."

"We can't do that!" Delanie was horrified at that, glaring at Don as he just laughed.

"We can. It's okay, sweetheart. If they knew that we were here, they would ask."

Abe stood back from his front door thirty minutes later. He was surprised to see Don but had been expecting him to drop in at some point. He shook hands with Don and then hugged Delanie, surprising her with that.

"Emma's out back. I know. It's raining but we've enclosed the porch and have windows that we close. It's very peaceful."

Darcy headed that way with Delanie in tow. Emma turned as she heard the footsteps and then stood, little Isaac heading for Darcy on a run. She was a favourite of his. Isaac then turned to Delanie and launched himself at her to the surprise of his mother.

"Isaac? Is that how you greet guests?" Emma couldn't control the smile as Isaac nodded. "And who do we have here, Darcy?"

"This is Don's Delanie. They were in town and apparently Don wanted to talk with you and Abe."

"And I need to talk to them. Delanie, it is so nice to meet you. Come. Have a seat. Tell me about yourself."

———

Delanie was soon wrapped up in conversation and laughter with the two ladies. Don watched for a moment before he turned to Doug and Abe. He knew that the two men were cousins and had each gone through some pretty hard stuff during what was classed as their adventures.

"Don, what can you tell us?" Abe watched with compassion as Don's face tightened for a moment.

Don nodded and then proceeded to tell the two exactly what had been going on with Delanie and himself. Doug reached for paper and pen to take notes. He saw Abe doing the same.

"Your house? It was definitely a bomb and not the gas to the grill?" Abe was thinking through what had happened.

"It was a bomb, set near the grill. I just couldn't walk up to it. I just dropped the meat and ran, grabbing Delanie as we ran." He grinned for a moment. "She had our cat in her arms and didn't drop her even when we hit the ground."

The two other men laughed, knowing how important animals could be to the ladies.

"What else?"

"We're finding that some of the teams coming in are not who they say they are. We're having to dig deeper into their backgrounds."

"That is something that you have to do. We had to." Abe sat back, his eyes on his notes. "What can we do for you?"

"It is difficult, Abe, when it's you. It's one thing for it to be one of the team or a friend or even a stranger. When it's the lady who you love, it makes it that much worse." Don rubbed at his face. "How do I keep Delanie safe and find whoever this is?"

"That's always a difficult problem, Don." Doug studied his friend. "You know our story, how Darcy was targeted by law enforcement. For you? That could be what you are facing. You are too careful with your life and your work."

"I try to be. My team is hurting, not just for this. They went through so much of their own."

"They did. My team's the same." Abe sat back, trying to come up with a plan. He finally spoke, his words catching at Don's ears and he listened closely to what Abe was suggesting.

Don finally nodded, Doug agreeing as well. Abe had had suggestions for how to protect Delanie, which Don had not considered, and also suggestions for how to draw out the person or persons involved.

Chapter 22

Delanie was happy, her face wreathed in smiles. Don just grinned at her as he tucked her into his truck to head for home. It had been a good decision, he decided, to head this way today. They had both needed this. Delanie had not said much but he could tell that it had helped her to speak with the two ladies and then the two men.

"Happy?" He continued to grin at her as he pulled away from Abe's home.

"I am. Thank you, Don. This is what we both needed." Delanie laid a hand on his arm. "We need to do this more often."

"We do. Abe mentioned that as well." Don headed for home, watching carefully for anyone following them.

"Do we have a tail?" Delanie turned to look behind her.

"Not that I can tell but that doesn't mean that someone isn't there." Don yawned, suddenly tired. The events with his team and now this with Delanie had tried his stamina greatly. He wasn't sleeping well right now, wanting to stay away and guard Delanie.

"You need to sleep, Don." Delanie watched him closely.

"I know that I do, sweetheart. It's hard. I need to stay away and defend you."

"I know that, Don. But God is in control. We do what we can to protect each other but we can't take His place. He has a plan for our lives that we are working through. We just keep our hands in His and trust Him to keep us under His wings."

Don nodded. Delanie was correct. That is what they were trying to do and it was very hard. As humans, they wanted to run ahead of God and they just couldn't do that.

The next day, Gideon, their minister, watched as Don and Delanie walked towards him. He was worried about the couple. He had had a chance to talk briefly with Don but he still worried and wanted answers from the couple.

"Gideon?" Don grinned at him. "Has anyone asked you to share a meal with them today?"

Gideon shook his head even as he returned the grin. Delanie stared at him and then at Don, her face shuttered for a moment. Gideon had always had trouble reading her. He had prayed that this would change now that she was married to a good friend of his.

"No, actually they haven't. I was going to ask you two to come for a meal." Gideon waited patiently for Don and Delanie to respond.

Don had turned to Delanie, waiting patiently for her to decide. He really wanted to spend time with his friend but he would wait for Delanie to make her decision.

Delanie sighed to herself. She knew what Don was up to. He wanted her to make the decision. That was not fair to him, she knew. She refused to make all the decisions that he wanted her to make. They were a team, she had decided, and needed to work together.

"You decide, Don. I'm fine with whatever your decision is." Delanie knew what Don wanted to do.

"Then, I guess we'll accept, Gideon. It's been a while since we shared a meal." Don followed Gideon from the church, waiting as he locked it up. "Did you walk today?"

"I did. I needed some God time before church." Gideon lived near the church and walked when he could.

Gideon watched Delanie closely over the meal. She participated to a certain degree but she still was hesitant, he thought, to fully engage in conversation. He prayed for her and for Don as well.

"Delanie? You said that you were from way up north. Tell me about your life there." Gideon saw Don shoot him a quick glance.

"There's not much to tell. I never felt wanted by;'+/ my family. They never went to church, not my parents and not my sisters. A friend started me going when I was young. I was not accepted by my family. I always felt like an outsider. And they never did anything to change that. My church family was great. They took me in. As to my education, I left there when I turned eighteen, moved here, graduated from college, and then set up my business." Delanie blinked quickly.

"Do you think there is something from there doing this? Or is it directed at Don?"

Don nodded. Delanie had expressed what they both thought and had briefly discussed. Gideon had a way of getting people to talk. He also knew that Gideon did not ask questions lightly or without having prayed for them.

Gideon watched the pair, knowing that he needed to answer but not sure if his answers would help.

"It may be that it is directed at you. It may also be that it is directed at Don. Or it could be the two of you. I know that your team feels that something was left over after the attackers were caught."

"We do. There has always been something with each one of them not explained by what the reason was for the attack on them." Don shook his head. "I just don't get it. I have never harmed anyone. At least, I haven't to my knowledge."

"No, it's not your nature to do that. And Delanie, I don't think that it's in your nature. Someone has decided that you both need to pay for something. We just need to figure it out."

Delanie had leaned forward with her arms on the table as Gideon spoke. She nodded at his words.

"And how do we do that, Gideon? How do we find them before they kill us?" Delanie's fear was just that.

"It's difficult to be in this situation, Delanie. Don has been there for so many people over the years.

He has a wealth of experience. I gather that you have likely spoken with Richard and Abe?" Don nodded at that question. "And they both would have given you lots of information and suggestions. Now, how do I help? Besides the obvious, of course." Gideon grinned at them both.

"Praying for us is helping, Gideon. We can't thank you enough for that. As to what else you can do? That's a good question."

Delanie frowned at Gideon for a moment.

"Gideon? Who can you reach out to? I mean, reach out to find information. They may speak with you rather than one of us or a police officer."

Gideon nodded. Delanie had asked what he had already put in place.

"I'm working on that, Delanie. If anyone contacts me or gives me any information at all, no matter how minute, I will pass it on to you. That's a given. Now, you're wanting to get on your way. Let me pray with you before you take off."

Chapter 23

Don's team waited for him on Monday, frowning when he didn't appear. They didn't have a team in for training but were planning on training themselves. It was very unusual for Don not to appear.

Mark walked back out of the building and looked towards where Don and Delanie were living. He had spoken with Daci the night before and she didn't seem to think that anything was amiss. But for Don not to show up? That was unusual. And for him not to answer phone calls or text messages? That was also unusual.

Thomas and Caleb ran for Thomas' truck, heading for Don's. His truck was there as was Delanie's car. They frowned at each other before they were out of the truck and running for the house. Thomas headed for the front door as Caleb searched outside

Pounding at the door, Thomas waited, afraid for his friends. Were they there or were they missing?

Don looked up at the sound of the pounding at the door. He rose, staggering for a moment. He had not slept the night before and had dosed off as he sat at the kitchen table. Delanie had finally drifted off. She had been terrified the night before and Don just would not walk away from her to seek his rest.

"Thomas?" Don stepped outside, squinting at Thomas.

"We were worried about you, Don. You weren't at the office." Thomas studied Don, seeing how rough he looked. "You haven't slept."

Don shook his head, watching as Caleb walked up the steps to the front porch.

"No, I didn't. Delanie couldn't sleep. She was absolutely terrified and we can't figure out why. Something is off somewhere." Don turned back towards the house, stopping as Thomas laid a hand on his arm. "Thomas?"

"How be you head over to the office? We'll look around." Thomas didn't back down from him, knowing that was what they had to do.

Don nodded, knowing that was what he had to do. He turned back into the house, slipped into his sneakers, and then headed for Delanie. He slipped on her shoes and then gathered her close. He walked out of the house and to his truck and slid her onto the seat, fastening the seatbelt around her. Don turned to stare at the house, knowing that something was wrong.

"Don?" Thomas had followed him and spoke quietly.

"Pack up our things, Thomas, and bring them to the office. We don't have a lot. Just watch her glass angel. She needs that reminder that there are angels all around us."

Caleb had already begun his search outside as Thomas moved back into the house. Thomas packed up Don and Delanie's belongings and placed them into his truck. He was saddened. They really didn't have much now. Don had said that they only had what they needed for now until they made some decisions.

Thomas walked back towards Caleb finding Caleb heading his way. Caleb was angry, Thomas could tell.

"Caleb?"

"Thomas? We need Toryn out here as well as either Aidan or George. Delanie was correct to be terrified." Caleb pointed back towards the house. "Someone was around in the night. The security cameras are damaged so that won't help us track who they were."

Thomas's face grew grim as he pulled out his phone and made the call to Toryn. Aidan was in court that day but Toryn promised to be there with George and other officers and crime scene techs. His only question was if Don and Delanie were safe.

Don walked away from his office. Delanie was stretched out on the couch. He had stood and watched her sleep after he had covered her with a soft yellow blanket. He was afraid for her, afraid that he would not be able to protect her. Don had no idea why she had been like she was the night before but he knew her well enough to know that there was a reason.

Toryn watched the activity around the house, his face stern. He had sent Thomas and Caleb back to the office, knowing that they needed to be around Don and set up security for the couple.

George walked towards him, evidence bags in his hands. He was disturbed to say the least. Whoever it was had just ramped up the assaults against Don.

"They placed a lot of cameras and microphones, Toryn. And it looks as if they weren't finished." George stared at the electronics in the bags. "They are really trying to find out what Don and Delanie are up to. I'm afraid for them."

"I am as well." Toryn bent over slightly to look at the bags. "And there won't be any evidence on them."

"That's what we think. They're careful that way. They're doing this but we have no further information to move the investigation forward. Emma's having trouble finding out who is it and that is very unusual for her."

"It is." Toryn rubbed at his cheek, trying to come to some understanding of what was going on. "We need to meet with Aidan and Lyle. There has to be something that we can determine."

"Darcy has sent on an email." George held up his phone. "She said that it's a profile. And she is usually right on with those."

"She is. She doesn't do that now except for friends. Law enforcement lost a valuable tool in their fight against crime when she was forced out by the rogue cop." Toryn walked away, praying that Darcy's profile would help. Other than that? He had no idea what to think or how to proceed.

Don turned to the conference room, a mug of coffee in his hand before it was set to one side. He read the information on the boards and then reached for a marker. He made his own notes from what he and Delanie had spent hours talking about. He wanted this over and over now for his love. And that didn't seem to be happening.

His men watched him and then approached, stopping him in his tracks. They simply prayed for him, knowing that was what they could do then. Their ladies were on the way as was Daci. They planned on spending the day, not in training but in investigating this. They just hoped that they could discover something that day that would break the case wide open.

Chapter 24

Delanie was angry. She had insisted that she needed to be in her office. Don had stared at her before she just walked away, blinking back her tears. She needed his support and didn't think that she had it. Daci stared between her and Don before she was beside her, an arm around her.

"Don doesn't want to take you into town?" Daci's voice held slight amusement.

"I didn't ask. He needs to be here to work on this." Delanie stared out of a window in the reception area. "And I need to keep my appointments. The kids depend on me." She didn't see Don standing in the doorway, Daci sending him a questioning look.

"I can take you in, if you like." Daci volunteered, knowing that Don was waiting for Delanie to speak.

"It's too dangerous for you, Daci. I'll just call and cancel them." Delanie was saddened and frustrated.

"It's okay, sweetheart. I'll take you in." Don wrapped her into his arms. "You're needing to go now."

"I am but I don't want to take you away from here. You're working on something." Delanie refused to look up at him.

"Nothing is as important as you are." Don hesitated, not sure how to proceed. "You need me with you. I get that. And I will be there. Now, let's head into town." He turned as Thomas and Mark approached. "Guys?"

"We're driving you, Don. For now, you have a chauffeur." Thomas shook his head, a grim look on his face.

"I see. Then, let's head out. Delanie? Do you need to take anything with you?"

Delanie shook her head, sharing a look with Daci who simply grinned at her.

"No, I don't think so. Everything I need is locked up at the office."

Twenty minutes later, Delanie stared in horror at her office. The front door had been broken down. She moved to walk that way, finding Don's arms around her to stop her.

"Don? I need to go in there." Delanie struggled to escape his hug and was unable to do that.

"No, sweetheart. You can't. We need to have the police go through it." Don's head turned as he heard car tires and saw George walking towards him from his car. "George is here. He'll go through your office and then come and find you."

George shared a look with Don and then studied Delanie. He could see the fear and agitation in her. He sighed. He had reached out to Aidan who was on his way. George walked towards the building, hesitating for a moment before he entered.

He was back in less than ten minutes, heading towards where Aidan had just arrived. The two detectives stood and watched the couple. Their discussion was troubled.

Aidan walked towards Don and Delanie, George heading for his car to call in a crime scene team.

"Don? Delanie? When were you last here?" Aidan stopped beside them.

"Friday afternoon, Aidan. I had appointments into the late afternoon. I know that I locked up and set the security system." Delanie leaned back against Don. "What happened here?"

"We'll walk you through once the techs are done. I haven't seen it. I don't know how damaged it is or isn't." Aidan walked away after that, heading for the office.

Thomas and Mark had stood back by Mark's truck, watching the activity. They shared a look as Don and Delanie headed back their way.

"Don? What's going on?"

"A break-in as you can see. We'll walk through soon. Delanie doesn't need this." Don tucked her away into the truck, the men standing in such a way as to keep an eye on her, the office building, and anyone who might be around. They knew that this was a dangerous time for them.

Aidan walked towards Don an hour later. George had had to leave to head for another crime scene. Aidan stopped for a moment in front of Don before he looked over at Delanie. Her face was shuttered as she watched the activity.

"Don? We can walk Delanie through the building." Aidan didn't say anything more.

Don reached for Delanie's hand and walked with her towards her office. Neither one was sure what to expect when they entered. Delanie walked through the office building, a frown on her face. Nothing was moved. Nothing was destroyed. And Aidan said that nothing was hidden in the building. She didn't understand why.

"Aidan? What can you tell us?" Don watched his bride closely.

"Not a lot. This is strange. It's as if someone broke in and then just walked through the building."

"And left no evidence." Don nodded. It was a scare tactic, he knew.

"This is meant to scare Delanie." Aidan watched her as she stood in the centre of her office, arms wrapped around herself. "She can't give up her office. She's filling a need that's out there. We can't have her shut down her office."

"No, we can't. We just have to come up with a way to keep her safe while she's here."

"And we will. I know that your team will want to be involved." Aidan looked up as Delanie made a sound. "Delanie?"

"I know that's necessary, Aidan. I just don't have to like it. And I don't. Don's team needs to be where they are, not with me." Delanie walked away, not looking back at the men. She sat, her mind already on what needed to be done that day.

———

Aidan watched her before he shook his head and walked away. He couldn't do anything. He had to leave that up to Don.

Don perched on the corner of her desk, his arms folded across his chest. He didn't speak. He didn't know what to say or how to encourage her. All he could do was pray for his bride and beg God to keep her safe. He wasn't ready to lose her yet.

"Don? What is your take on this?" Delanie sat back, her eyes on Don.

Don shrugged.

"I'm not sure, sweetheart. I am really not sure. For today, I'm here with you. I can work from here. Thomas and Mark will be back to pick us up. We'll need to find somewhere else to stay, given what they would around the house."

"I know. I hate this. This is putting so many of your friends at risk."

"Your friends as well, sweetheart. They consider you a friend and want this over for you. We just don't have the key to unlock the mystery."

"And I pray that we find that before someone is injured or killed. And we can't protect ourselves that well, now can we?" Delanie didn't expect a response. There just wasn't a way to do that, she knew.

Chapter 25

Delanie paced the motel room that Don had found for them. He hadn't wanted to head for his parents, as much as they had asked them to. And Daci? It wasn't that she hadn't offered. It was just that he felt such a sense of danger around them. She was worried. Don had wrapped her into a hug and kissed her before he left to find food for them. That had been an hour ago. And he had not returned.

Stopping every few moments, Delanie stood to one side of the window and pushed the drape back enough to peek out. Don's truck wasn't out there. She had thought that she had heard it park in front of the door thirty minutes ago. But Don had not knocked at the door.

Worried about Don, Delanie continued to pace and pray, begging God to let Don tap at the door. It just didn't happen. She reached for her phone and scrolled through her messages. She found the one from just after he had left, simply stating that he wouldn't be long and that he loved her.

Delanie set her phone aside and sat, her arms wrapped around herself. She didn't know where Don was but she knew that he was in danger. She just didn't know how to help him. Delanie jumped as her phone rang and she reached for it, fear in her eye.

"Hello?" She breathed a sigh of relief. It was Deree.

"Delanie? How are you? We've been worried about you." Deree shared a look with David. Neither one of Don's parents had been able to sleep.

"I don't know. Don went to get food and hasn't come back." Delanie struggled to control her tears. She didn't weep, not ever, and felt that was all she had done or wanted to do in the last few weeks. The stress was wearing her down.

"He hasn't? Have you called for help?" David spoke up.

"Not yet. I should." Delanie didn't say good bye as she hung up, leaving Deree and David to stare at one another. She stared at her phone before she called Aidan.

To say that Aidan was shocked to hear from Delanie would be somewhat of an understatement. And then to hear that Don had left to grab them a meal and not returned? He was out of his office and running to his car. Don would not just do that. That was not the character of the man to walk away from his bride who he loved deeply. Everyone could see the love between the couple.

Aidan walked towards the motel room, watching closely for any sign of Don. The heavy rain and the darkness were not what he wanted right at that moment. All he could do was pray for his friend and that he had returned by this time. He tapped at the door, calling quietly for Delanie and telling her that he was there.

Delanie froze in front of the door as she heard the tap, her hand on her neck. As she heard Aidan's voice, she still didn't move until he tapped again and called for her, a more urgent sound to his voice. She flew at the door, fumbling as she unlocked the door and pulled it open. Her eyes were huge with fear and worry as Aidan entered.

"Delanie? Any word?" Aidan's hands on her arms kept her upright as she stumbled to move out of his way.

Delanie's head was shaking. She didn't know where Don was and that terrified her.

"He hasn't. It's been too long, Aidan. He would have called me to let me know that he was delayed. The only text that I got from him was just after he left. He said that he wouldn't be long and that he loved me." Delanie backed away until her legs hit the bed and she sat down abruptly.

"No word? Okay. Do you know where he was heading?"

"No, I don't. I think it was for fast food but I'm not sure. He didn't say." Delanie buried her face in her hands. "How do we find him?"

Aidan walked out of the room and headed for the patrol vehicle that had appeared, its emergency lights flashing eerily through the rain and darkness.

"Aidan? What's up?" Tom, the officer, pulled his slicker on as he stepped out of the vehicle.

"Don's missing and has been for more than an hour. Delanie said that he went to grab them food and hasn't come back." Aidan stared back at the motel room door. "She's frantic and terrified."

"I can only imagine how she is feeling." Tom stared around. "It's going to be impossible to find any trace of him in this weather if he did get back here."

"I know. Call in help and see what you can find. I'm finding someone to be with Delanie and it's not going to be family." Aidan walked away and back to his car. He simply called in and asked for a female patrol officer to come and stay with Delanie. That was all that he could do for now.

Searching the area didn't result in any good news. They just couldn't tell if Don had returned and then disappeared from there. Aidan ensured that the description and plate number for Don't true went out to all the patrol officers. He shrugged deeper into his jacket. The temperature was dropping and the rain made it very damp and chilly.

Delanie paced the room, not watching the female patrol officer who stood in front of the door, watching Delanie in return. She had spoken with Aidan a bit ago and had been discouraged by his words. Don was missing and they had no idea where he was.

David and Deree walked towards Aidan, Daci running to catch up with them. He simply pointed them towards the motel room. The officer stepped to one side as she opened the door to let them in. Deree took one look at Delanie and then swept her into her arms, her mother hug breaking through the barrier that Delanie had tried to erect to protect herself. Delanie began to sob, clinging to her mother-in-law.

David turned and walked out of the room, heading for Aidan. Aidan waited for him to approach.

"Aidan? Any word?" David peered through the darkness. The rain had stopped, Worthing that they were all grateful for.

"Not a word. We're looking but we can't tell if he made it back here and then disappeared. The motel doesn't have security cameras which is surprising."

"It is." David hesitated. "Where do we start to look? And I assume that you have reached out to the team."

"We have. They haven't seen him since they left the office building. They're all involved in training tomorrow so they aren't able to help us. That's frustrating for them." Aidan turned as he heard a shout and then ran towards the officer waving at him.

David watched him leave and then stood, his face turned up to the sky. *Lord, where is my boy? Where do we search? Protect and defend him, Lord, wherever he is. Comfort Delanie and help her to find the strength and peace she needs at this time.*

———

Chapter 26

A day passed with Don still missing. Deree had insisted that Delanie move in with them for the time being. Delanie had just refused, stating that she needed to be where Don had left her so that he could find her. She didn't sleep and was unable to, in fact. She simply stared at the door, waiting for Don to walk through it.

Aidan was puzzled. There had been no sign of Don. They had been back around the motel and the businesses. Security camera feeds were accessed but they were of little help in their investigation. The weather was just too bad for anything to show up other than lights.

Then late that afternoon, Aidan ran for his car, heading for a business on the opposite side of town at a neglected business. He slammed on the brakes, shoved open his door, and then ran, the door slamming behind him.

His feet pounded across the broken and overgrown pavement. The patrol officer stood up from where he had been crouching down behind an abandoned dumpster.

"Fred? What do you have?"

"Don. I stopped in here just to cover everything. A street person pointed this way, telling me that he thought the man was dead." A frown covered Fred's face. "It's Don. He's alive but he's in rough shape."

Aidan nodded as he moved rapidly forward and then knelt beside Don. His hand checked for a pulse and respiration. He breathed a sigh of relief that Don was still alive.

"You called it in?"

"I did. The paramedics are on the way." Fred waved at the paramedics and directed them to where Aidan had risen to his feet.

The paramedics worked rapidly on Don, surprised to find him in such a desolate place. Don was well known to the emergency services, willing to help them out in any way that he could.

"Fellows? What are his injuries?" Aidan moved closely, crouching down beside them.

"Exposure is the big one. He's been beaten as well. How long has he been missing and out here?"

"About twenty-four hours. His wife called it in when he didn't return from grabbing a meal for them. That had been about an hour."

"His wife? I didn't know that he had married." The senior paramedic adjusted the intravenous flow.

"It's a story in itself. It really hasn't been that long." Aidan stood and paced away, motioning Fred with him. "Stay with him, Fred. I'll bring in Delanie and then contact his parents and Daci."

Aidan pulled into the motel parking lot and stopped in front of the room where Delanie was still ensconced. She had just refused to leave. He studied the door, knowing that while Don was found, he was still in critical condition. He walked towards the door and tapped on it.

Delanie raised her head from the pillow. She had finally laid down but not to sleep. She had spent the time in prayer. On her feet, Delanie headed for the door and opened it, staring at Aidan.

"Aidan? I didn't expect to see you." She frowned at him.

"We found Don, Delanie. Grab what you need and I'll take you to him." Aidan waited patiently as Delanie stared at him and then spun to pack their belongings and grab her purse. He reached for the packs, knowing that Delanie would not come back there. He watched as she headed for the office and then back towards him, leaving the key with the attendant.

"Where did you find him?"

"Behind a dumpster on the other side of town. It was at an abandoned building. A patrol officer found him." Aidan didn't tell her what the officer had been told. That would come at a later time.

Delanie shifted on her seat in the waiting room at the hospital. Aidan had left her there and under police guard as he walked through to the examination rooms. He decided that he had been doing this far too many times for his friends. When would it stop, he wondered? And then he began to pray for his friends.

Caleb had been freed up by the team and sent to be with Delanie. He had collected Cullea on the way in, knowing that his wife would want to be there. Cullea sat quietly beside Delanie, praying for her friends, begging in fact that Don would be okay. Not much information was available to them. Delanie had shaken her head when Caleb had crouched down in front of her and asked her what she knew. Her emotions were raw enough that she didn't think that she could control her tears if she spoke.

David, Deree, and Daci arrived, heading for Delanie. Deree had sat beside her as well, an arm around her, an audible prayer sounding in the younger woman's ears.

Turning to find Caleb, David pointed to the outside. Caleb nodded, knowing that David would want to know everything that he could tell him. Not that there was a lot, Caleb decided. Aidan had not given much information other than that Don was found and at the hospital receiving treatment and that he was heading that way with Delanie.

"What do you know, Caleb?" David paused just outside the door, watching the movement of pedestrians around them.

"Not a lot, David. Aidan didn't say much other than that he had found Don and Don was at the hospital for treatment. He had been heading in with Delanie at that point."

David nodded, knowing that Aidan would not say much until he had spoken with Don. He just prayed that he would be able to do that and soon. Night had fallen and David was exhausted, just as he knew that the others were.

"The others are heading this way?"

"Not right now. I'll stay until we find out something. They and their ladies are working this, to see what they can come up with. They're working the profile that Darcy gave Don." Caleb was troubled. He was also torn. He wanted to stay here with Delanie but he also wanted to be there in the thick of the investigations.

David nodded, knowing how Caleb would feel. He turned as he felt a hand on his back. Gideon stood there, worry on his face.

"David? Is it true? Don is here?"

"It is, Gideon. Thank you for coming."

"Delanie called me, telling me what happened and that Don was here. I wasn't sure that I had heard her correctly. She was crying that hard."

"He's here. We don't have a lot of information yet. Come in with me. We need to pray with the ladies." David and Gideon walked away, leaving Caleb staring at the night sky, not counting the stars that were appearing.

Chapter 27

Rising as the physician motioned to her, Delanie walked towards him, feeling Deree and David with her. Daci had stayed seated, knowing that her father would be back as soon as he could to find her. Gideon claimed Delanie's chair.

"Daci? You're okay?"

"I'm not sure, Gideon. I am really not sure. This is so worrying. I wish that it was all over and whoever is responsible was under arrest." Daci was angry.

"I know. We all do. We're praying for them but it's tough to stand on the sidelines and not become more involved." Gideon gave her a small smile.

"That's what it is, isn't it? Standing on the sidelines and not able to get into the game. Just because it's not us. But we still worry about them and fear for them and pray for them." Daci's eyes closed for a moment as she fought back tears.

"That's what we do, Daci. You've done that with the other five. They've all talked with me." Gideon would say no more.

"I figured that they had. How do we do this? How do we solve this?"

Caleb had been listening to Daci, knowing that she was speaking her frustrations.

"We pray, as Gideon has said. We keep working through what we have. The whiteboards are filling at the office, or so I'm told. Emma is firing off information as fast as she can to us and to Aidan. Abe and Richard are weighing in on how to keep Don and Delanie safe. And that extends to you and your parents, Daci. We are learning more about Delanie's family but we need to speak with her first. That's not happening today."

"No, her attention is on Don, as it should be." Daci bit at her lip. "What if it's not Don at all? What if it's to get to someone else? Not Dad or Mom. But what if he's being used to get at one of the emergency services?"

Aidan had been listening to Daci from where he stood just out of sight of her. His eyes closed. That was one possibility that he didn't know if they had thought through. Footsteps stopped beside him. Toryn looked between Aidan and then the group.

"Aidan? Care to explain the look on your face?" Toryn kept his voice low.

"I would. Daci asked what if it wasn't Don. What if it was directed at emergency services?"

Toryn nodded. He had had a long talk with the police chiefs in both Riverville and Elmton. Both Caleb Logan from the first town and his friend from Elmton, Andrew McBeth, had asked about that. The towns had faced that scenario not that long before except that time it was the emergency services used to go after Doug's wife, Darcy.

"It's possible, Aidan. Someone with a grudge from years ago has chosen to go after Don just because he has a security team. And because of that fact, they are going to go after the police services here."

"That's what I am just beginning to see. How do we ever find them?" Aidan rubbed at his face, the thought worrying him.

"I'll talk to Lyle and see what we can come up with. We may need to pull you from every other case and do this only." Toryn walked away, troubled at that very thought.

Aidan walked over to sit beside Gideon, his eyes on the couple who hesitated in the doorway. He frowned. They were strangers and were hesitant to be there. He was on his feet and walking towards him when they turned and left. His phone was out as he followed them and he took photos of them. They wanted something, he decided.

Caleb had followed him, a frown on his own face. He looked between Aidan and the departing couple.

"Do you know them, Aidan?"

"No, I don't. They wanted something or were looking for someone. I wonder?" Aidan turned to stare back at the hospital. "Delanie's parents wouldn't have just shown up, would they?"

Caleb shrugged.

"I have no idea. Do we have a photo of her parents?"

Aidan nodded, pulling Caleb to one side. He pulled out his phone and then turned to his work photos. He searched for one and then held it up to show the other man.

Caleb sighed. Delanie's parents were in town. He just wanted to know how they found her and then knew that she was at the hospital.

"We need to find out how they knew. Delanie has not had any contact with them since she left home. She went to school here." Caleb could feel the anger beginning to build inside him. The stress of the team going through life and death situations had drained them all. The team just wanted it all over with.

Delanie hesitated in the doorway to the examination room, her eyes on the room and the equipment before she looked at the bed. A strangled sob rose within her before she was across the room. She stood for a moment, her eyes on Don. Delanie bent over the stretcher, a hand on Don's face. She stared at Don, seeing the whiteness of his face and the dark circles under his eyes.

Deree and David stood on either side of Delanie, shocked at their son's appearance. They had been warned that he would look rough. They had not expected him to be in that bad of shape.

There were footsteps on the floor that sounded loudly in the silence and then stopped on the other side of the bed. The physician watched Delanie carefully, seeing the stress and worry that she was trying hard to hide.

"Delanie? May I call you that?"

Delanie jumped and looked up in fright. David's arm went around her shoulders and hugged her.

"You can. Don? What's going on with him?"

"He's in rough shape, Delanie. I won't hide that from you. He was out in the elements for close to twenty-four hours from what we can determine. That has caused some concern. He was also beaten. There are no broken bones or anything like that. We are waiting for him to rouse so that we can assess him properly."

"And when will that be?" Delanie drew in a deep breath. She felt Deree's arm around her as well. She needed that support.

"We don't know, Delanie. We are moving him up to a room on the floor shortly. You can stay with him for now."

David shared a looked with Deree before he walked away. He was deeply worried about his son. He looked up as Caleb and Aidan flanked him.

"David? What's the word on Don?" Caleb shared a worried look with Aidan.

"He's still unconscious but they're moving him to a room on a floor. They are concerned about a concussion. Who did this? Aidan, find them and make them pay." David walked away, vengeance warring with worry for his son.

Chapter 28

Late that night, Delanie still stood beside Don's bed. He had not roused at all. That worried her to no end. Her hand rested on his cheek, feeling the stubble on it that scraped against her hand. She looked around and then simply crawled up beside him. Her head rested on his shoulder and an arm was wrapped around him.

Delanie slept, not hearing the nurses as they came in and out. One had stopped beside the bed and then found a blanket to cover her up. She smiled sadly, knowing that the pair were still in danger.

Don's eyes flickered open and closed early the next morning. He felt warm, he decided, and comfortable. He turned his head slightly, feeling Delanie's hair as it brushed against his face. He smiled slightly, a hand raised to rest on her arm. He slept again, this time dropping into sleep and not unconsciousness.

Thomas walked towards Caleb an hour later. Caleb had refused to leave the waiting room, staying on watch overnight. The team had agreed to that. Thomas had promised to take over for him and had shown up earlier than Caleb had expected.

"Caleb? How is he?" Thomas sat beside his friend, handing over the cup of coffee and muffin that he had brought for him.

Caleb took the food with thanks. He shot a look towards the room before he shook his head.

"The nurse said that he's sleeping right now. Delanie apparently crawled up beside him to sleep. I could see our ladies doing the same." Caleb grinned as Thomas laughed.

"That they would. Any word from Aidan?"

Caleb shook his head. Aidan was off that day, he knew. That meant that Delanie would not be updated on where the investigation stood.

"He's off today. George is around, Aidan said, but they're overwhelmed with cases." Caleb shared a look with Thomas. "That sounds too familiar."

"It does. I think someone is setting Don up for a fall. And we need to prevent that. Are Richard and Abe around?"

"They'll be here this afternoon. As to the team? Thomas, Paul, and Joshua are training?"

"They are. You're to go home and get some sleep. We just cut back on what we're training on. The team leader was fine with that. He knows Don from high school, he said."

"He does? Who doesn't Don know?" Caleb rose and stretched before he walked away.

Thomas watched his friend walk away and then turned his attention back to Don's room. He rose and walked that way, standing just inside the door. His attention was on the bed before he heard footsteps beside him. The physician was there, frowning.

"Did she do that?" He was puzzled at finding Delanie on the bed beside Don.

"She did. They need that contact, Doc. They're in a life and death situation and need to have one another close to them." Thomas was adamant about that.

The physician nodded and then walked over to assess Don. He stood back for a moment before he made his notes on the chart. He walked away, turning for a moment to study Don and then Delanie. The physician could feel the presence of God in the room. He didn't believe in angels but decided that just perhaps that is what God did. He was a nominal Christian but knew that he would be looking into it further.

Thomas watched the physician walk away before he headed back for the waiting room and sat, a frown on his face. He wasn't sure where the investigation was heading but they really didn't seem to be making any progress. A chime from his phone drew his attention. Emma had sent a text, asking for Thomas to check his emails when he could.

Delanie roused an hour later, her eyes on Don. He had turned his face towards her during the night and she studied it. It was not quite as white as it had been and the dark circles were not quite as prominent. She dropped a kiss on his cheek and then slipped away from the room. Delanie stared back at him and then walked towards where Thomas had risen to wait for her.

"Delanie? You okay?" Thomas pointed to a seat.

"I don't know, Thomas. I really don't know." She looked up as Daci appeared, hugging her, and then taking with thanks the food that Daci handed her. "I need this, Daci. Thanks so much."

"How is Don?" Daci had spent the night awake and praying for her brother.

"He is sleeping, I think. He looks better. I need to talk with the physician." Delanie's eyes closed for a moment as a tear trickled down her cheek. "How do we do this? How do we find out who it is that is behind this?"

Thomas bit at his lip. Caleb had sent on the photo of the couple from the night before. They needed to confirm with Delanie whether or not she knew them.

"Delanie? I need to show you a photo of a couple who showed up downstairs last night. Tell me if you recognize them." Thomas handed over his phone.

Delanie took it and looked at him, not sure what to expect. Her eyes dropped to the photo. Thomas and Daci watched as shock, then fear, and then worry crossed her face.

"Delanie?" Thomas's hand reached to rest on her arm. "Talk to us. Who are the?"

"Not my parents. It's a couple who are their best friends. Or rather they were. I don't know if they still are. What are they doing here? How did they find me?" Delanie's face held her fear.

———

"I don't know. We've sent this on to Emma and she's working it. We'll keep you as safe as we can, Delanie. You know that."

Delanie nodded. "I know that you will do your best. But will that be enough?" She slumped back against the chair, sipping at the cup of coffee that she had picked up. "This is not making any sense. I can't see my parents doing this to either Don or myself. We were not connected until that day on the trail. Are they really after Don or me? Or are we just the ones that they chose to hide what they are really doing?"

Thomas shared a look with Daci who seemed surprised at Delanie's words.

"We wondered about that, Delanie. Toryn reached out to us last night. He and Aidan had a thought. They asked if we thought maybe that was the case. They are wondering if someone is after the emergency services and is using Don to cover that. He works closely with the services."

Delanie stared at him, hearing Daci's indrawn breath.

"Don and I talked about that on that nafternoon. We were tossing around ideas. That was one that he had and just couldn't let go of. So if that is the case, how do we do that? Can we prove it? Doug would be a good one to speak with, given what happened there."

"He would be. So would Caleb and Andrew." Thomas was on his feet, heading away from the ladies, his phone out to make a call. Richard was agreeable with their thoughts and would be there that afternoon.

His next call to Abe received the same reaction. They would meet and consider that.

Chapter 29

Delanie watched Thomas, knowing that he was making plans. Those plans might not be what she wanted to do but they were the experts in providing security. She knew them well enough to trust them.

"Daci? What are your thoughts?" Delanie shot the other lady a look.

"That this is the correct reason. Now we just have to figure out who and why." Daci reached for the notebook that she had in her purse. She pulled the cap from her pen and waited for Delanie to speak.

"So, who would you suspect? You've lived here for years."

"I have. And there are many who would be suspect. But there has to be someone who hates the services enough to do this. And that person likely pretends to support them."

"Then, start listing the Police Services Board and work out from there. Who is in charge of the other services? Who has contact with them on a regular basis for whatever reason?" Delanie leaned forward, her face thoughtful. "I think it is someone who had something happen and then has hidden their hatred and thirst for revenge for years. We can't defend against someone who is hidden. That's where God comes in. He is our Defender."

"That He is. I don't know how people do it that don't have faith. Now, as to the police board, these are the people." Daci continued to name people as she wrote them down. She didn't look up as Thomas sat back beside her, his head tilted to read her notes.

"You're listing a lot of names there, Daci." He grinned as she looked up.

"I know. I'm trying to remember everyone who has a connection to the board members." She sighed. "I'll run out of paper this way."

"Let me call Taran or one of the ladies. They can bring in a tablet or a laptop. That would work better."

"Thank you, Thomas. That will." Daci looked around as a physician approached Delanie.

"Delanie? Can we talk?" The physician sat beside Delanie, eyeing Thomas and Daci.

"You can. This is Don's sister, Daci, and one of his team members, Thomas. What can you tell me?"

"Don has roused enough that we can evaluate him. He does have a concussion which is to be expected given the beating that he took. He did have exposure as well. The soaking that he took didn't result in pneumonia. However, he will not be working for a while. Can his team manage that?"

Thomas nodded, knowing what the physician was asking.

"We can manage, Doc. The teams coming in for training know that we don't always offer everything each week. Don can work in the office and the rest of us will pick up what we need to. It's how we always do it. We don't go away any more for security purposes."

———

The physician was nodding, knowing Don and his team from church.

"I know that's what you do, Thomas. Now, Daci? Are you looking after Delanie?" He grinned at her.

"I am, Jack. That I am. As much as she will let me. So are Mom and Dad. How long will Don be in here?"

"A couple of days and then he can go home." He looked at Delanie as she drew in a sharp breath. "Delanie?"

"That's the problem, Jack. We don't have a home to go home to. Our home was destroyed a couple of days ago and then the one that we were in was targeted and we were forced to leave it."

"I see." Jack studied her and then Thomas. Thomas was watching Jack, knowing that Jack had houses that he rented out and that they all had strong security systems. Don's team had worked on that for him. "I have a house that is empty. It is furnished. It's yours for as long as you and Don need it at no rent." Jack's hand went up. "Don has been good to the people in this town and won't take anything in return. This is my thanks for it." He reached into his pocket for a business card and scrawled the address on the back of it. He handed it to Delanie. "Check it out and then come and see me. I'll have the keys for you." He walked away, leaving Delanie staring after him.

"It's a good house, Delanie. We've used it as a safe house in the past. So we do know it." Timothy stared at Delanie for a moment. "Let's get you back in to see Don and then I'll grab the keys from Jack. He'll have them with him. Don't ask how he knows. God works through him that way."

Delanie walked through the house, knowing that it was safe. She just didn't feel safe. She paused at a framed photo of an eagle soaring into a storm. *God, this is You. You have provided this for us. Thank you. Heal my fellow, please dear Lord. And help us to solve this before anyone else is hurt.*

Thomas walked back towards her from assessing the outside. Daci stood in the kitchen doorway and watched Delanie as well. That lady had a peace about her that puzzled Daci. She just shook her head as she heard Thomas speaking.

"Delanie? Will this do?"

"It will. Jack is wonderful, isn't he? And we will be safe, I gather, or as safe as we can be?"

"As safe as you can be. No place is totally safe and you are aware of that. Now, you'll need to do some shopping. I understand that Don is having tests done at the moment from what you said?"

"He is. I guess we go shopping." Delanie frowned. "Did anyone find Don's truck? It had some of our clothes in it."

"Not that I know of." Thomas shot off a quick text to Caleb, asking him to search that out. "Okay. So we go shopping. Daci? Are you needed in the office?"

Daci shook her head. Even if she was, she would postpone whatever it was to be there for Delanie. Delanie needed her.

———

"No, not for now. Let's get the shopping done and then head back for here and then to the hospital. I know how to shop and shop quickly." She grinned at Thomas as he shook a finger at her.

Chapter 30

Word had spread throughout Oak City that Don had been injured and was hospitalized. It also spread that his bride, Delanie, was in danger as well. People looked at one another and then around at the townspeople. It was felt by all that someone in town was the one responsible for this. And it was determined among them that they would help bring the ones who were responsible to justice.

Aidan was surprised by the amount of information that was waiting on his desk on the next day. He had just returned from a quick trip out of town and knew that he would have a pile of documents to go through. He quickly scanned through it, pausing at a folder. His hand rested on it, knowing that it would change the investigation.

Opening the folder, Aidan began to read. Emma had come through once more, he thought. His pen was out as he began to make notes. He sat back at last, his thoughts whirling. How did Emma find that information? She had confirmed their suspicions that someone from town was targeting the emergency services.

On his feet, Aidan looked for George and then for Toryn. He shut Toryn's office door before he sat. George kept glancing between Aidan and Toryn, not sure what was up.

Toryn studied Aidan. He's discovered something, he decided.

"Aidan? What did you find out?"

Aidan nodded. Now that he had George and Toryn with him, he wasn't sure how to proceed.

"I have found out something. Emma sent on some information that I need to go over with you. She's confirmed that someone is after the emergency services. She is still tracking down which one. She has indicated that she is on the trail of who it is but they have hidden themselves well." Aidan handed over the folder, knowing that Toryn would read through it and make his own decisions before he handed it over to George.

There was silence in the room as Toryn read through the paperwork and then handed the file to George. George read through it as well, amazed at the conclusions that Emma had come to.

"How does she do this?" George handed the folder back to Aidan.

"She can't explain it, George. Now, are we in agreement with this?"

"We are. I want you and George working on this. Hand off what you can of your cases." Toryn's phone receiver was in his hand as he called for Lyle to come to his office.

Lyle tapped at the door and entered, a frown on his face.

"Toryn? What's up?" He took the folder that Aidan was waving at him. He read through it, a deep breath coming from him when he finished reading. "How do we do this? Aidan, you and George?"

"I've already asked that Aidan and George concentrate on this. We need to reassign their cases."

"And that is being done. I had already had that thought to clear off their desks. How is Don involved in this?"

"I think that they decided to go after Don as a coverup for what they were really up to. I've heard rumblings once in a while about why Don and his team were targeted. I spoke with Doug Foster in Riverville to get his thoughts." Aidan grew thoughtful. "We went through this with Doug and Darcy. By this, it looks as if it is only the emergency services in Oak City. I suspect that they will ramp up their workings now."

"I agree. We need to ensure that Delanie is safe. They'll go after her to get to Don. His team and their ladies are safe. Don's parents and sister are safe." Lyle frowned at Aidan. "That couple? Was it her parents?"

Aidan shook his head. Thomas had sent him a text that informed him of Delanie's words.

"No, it's not. Apparently they are good friends of her parents. It doesn't explain how they found her. She has had no contact with her parents since she left there." Aidan was puzzled by that as well. "I have asked Emma to look into it."

"Thanks, Aidan. We'll need to do that as well." Lyle shared a look with Toryn. "This is going to get really bad for them and soon. We'll need to work up a protective unit for them."

"And we are doing that. We're vetting the volunteers right now. And there have been dozens of volunteers. Don is well thought of by our force."

"He is. Keep me updated, Aidan, George." Lyle was gone at that.

Aidan walked towards the waiting room in the hospital a short time later. He nodded at Thomas before he looked around for Delanie.

"She's with Don, Aidan." Thomas grinned at him.

"She is? Is he awake?"

"Not really. She just doesn't want to be apart from him. And I can understand that. She was terrified that night."

"She was." Aidan thought back to the night that Don disappeared. "Thankfully, he wasn't gone for long but it was long enough to play with her mind."

"It was. Now, how do we help?"

"By continuing what you are doing. You're sending me the information that you're finding. You're continuing with the work that Don has laid out for you. I know how worried you all are." Aidan paused, gathering his thoughts. "George and I are working on this and this alone. Have your team think through who it could be in town and sent it to me or George. And there are officers who will be around providing security. That's not an option. Your team can't be here all the time."

"No, we can't. That's what's worrying us. By the way, Abe and Richard are due in this afternoon.

We want to meet with them as a team and with you and George. Delanie has just told me that she will be there.”

“She will, will she?” Aidan grinned as he rose, heading for Don. He needed Don’s statement and he prayed that Don would be awake enough to do that.

Chapter 31

Delanie's hand rested on Don's cheek, seeking to soothe his agitation. His head was tossing and turning as he roused and that scared her. She didn't turn as she heard the door open, thinking that it was just a nurse. She was surprised to see Aidan standing at the end of the bed.

"Aidan? You're back."

"I am, Delanie. Has Don been awake fully yet?"

"Not yet but he is rousing. You need to talk to him." Sadness sounded in her voice.

"I do. We need to get his statement before he talks too much to anyone else." Aidan watched as Don's eyes opened and he glanced around. "Don?"

"Aidan? Where am I?"

"You're in the hospital, Don." Delanie reached for his hand, finding his grasping hers. "Aidan needs to talk with you."

"I can't remember anything, Aidan. I don't know what happened or why I'm here." Don's eyes closed and he slept once more.

Delanie gave a brief grin at Aidan as he shook his head.

"Does that count as a statement?"

"For now, it will. Call me if he awakens again. George and I are working on this and this only." His hand went up at her protest. "We think that this is

---

directed at the emergency services and we have to work on this and solve it to solve that."

"That's what I was going to ask. I think that I was just incidental to it all but because Don and I are a couple, they'll go after me to get to him." Delanie was sober as she spoke. "Isn't that how it goes?"

"It is. I'm sorry, Delanie. I wish that it was different. I mean, you and Don are the couple that are meant to be. Everyone can see that you each are God's choice for the other. It's just what you're going through. We all fear that it will get a lot worse than it already has."

"That's what I think, that it will get worse. How do I stay safe?"

Aidan and George had talked about that and had some plans. They just didn't know if the plans would work.

"We will do everything that we can to keep you safe. We will work with Don's team to do that. Abe and Richard have also been in touch as have the police chiefs from Riverville and Elmton. Thomas here has been in contact with other friends who will help. We will do our best." Aidan knew that he was not really reassuring her.

Delanie stared at him, not sure what to think or to say. She turned back to Don, finding her hand still grasped tightly in his. She sighed. There was no way that he was letting go of her.

———

"How do we decide who it is? And how do we find out the information that we need for you to arrest him?"

"We're working on that, Delanie. It is going to take time, unfortunately." Aidan walked away at last, not sure that he would be able to do that before Don or Delanie was targeted again.

Don roused later that evening, this time staying awake. He looked around the room, recognizing it as a hospital room. He frowned, trying to remember what happened that brought him there. He moved and felt the tug of the IV line to his hand.

Wanting to be on his feet, Don stared at the IV needle before he pulled it and then clamped the sheet over the site to stop the trickle of blood. He sat on the side of the bed, waiting for the dizziness to ease.

He searched for clothes and found them. He dressed as rapidly as he could before he walked towards the door. Don wasn't sure what he would find out there but he was certain that Delanie would be there. And he was correct. As soon as his footsteps sounded on the tiled floor, her head was raised and then she was running towards him, slowing enough not to knock him over when she threw herself into his arms.

Paul watched from the waiting room, shaking his head. He just had to do that, didn't he? He knew that Don would want to leave and headed for the nurse who stared at him. Paul just shrugged before he pointed down the hallway.

Delanie clung to Don, happy that he was on his feet but worried that he was doing too much.

"Don, should you be up?"

"I need to be, sweetheart. We need to move away from her." He swung her around with her hand tight in his. "Who's waiting for us?"

"Paul is. And we have a place to stay. Jack came through with a house." She walked slowly beside him, knowing that he was shaky on his feet.

"Jack did? And I have a good idea which one. Okay." He grinned down at her for a moment before he looked up at Paul who had come to stand before them. "Paul?"

"Just had to sneak away, didn't you?" Paul grinned. "I have your paperwork. Jack expected this. Come on. Let's get you to your for-now home."

"That sounds good. When are we meeting?"

"Tomorrow. The team has been meeting with Abe, Richard, Aidan, and George. For now, those two officers are working on this. There have been developments that we need to talk about."

"I see. Okay, Paul. Let's get us home then." Don swayed slightly on his feet before Paul's hand was around his arm to help him walk forward.

Don sank gratefully into a chair, unable to stand on his feet. Delanie watched him, worried that he had left the hospital too soon before she was across the room and kneeling beside him. He wrapped her into a hug, feeling the sobs shaking her body.

Paul turned back to the kitchen, troubled and sorry that the couple was facing this. He knew what it was like to a certain extent and didn't like it one bit.

———

165

He reached for the coffeepot to make them coffee and then for bread and sandwich fixings. Not one of them likely felt much like eating but they needed something, Don in particular.

Don's head went down on Delanie's as he dozed off, unable to help himself. Delanie raised herself up to a standing position, gently shoving Don back against the chair and reached for a blanket to cover him.

Delanie walked into the kitchen, worry for Don on her face. Paul pointed silently to a chair and she gratefully pulled it back and sat. She nodded as he set the food in front of her.

"Don's sleeping, Paul. I don't know that he should have come out yet." Delanie yawned herself.

"He wouldn't stay there, Delanie. There are too many people who could get hurt. And we can pull in security better here. There are officers outside right now." Paul sat as well, bowing his head to pray over their food. "We'll keep you as safe as we can."

"That's okay, Paul. I trust you to put in place the plans that we talked about. I just want this over. I want to know why someone would do what they have. Don hasn't hurt anyone and never would."

Chapter 32

The next morning, Don was on his feet early in the morning. His body hurt and so did his head. He had examined his face that morning, seeing faint bruising covering it. He didn't know what happened and that worried him. If he didn't know what happened, Don wasn't sure how he would ever protect Delanie. And that he wanted to as much as he needed to breathe.

Delanie approached him from behind, standing for a moment to study him. She sighed. He wasn't hurting more than he would admit, she acknowledged to herself. She simply moved towards him and wrapped her arms around him.

Don jumped and then wrapped her into his arms. He felt the sobs that shook her body and wet his shirt. His own tears wet her hair. How long they stood there, they were never sure. A knock at the door roused them and Don kissed her before letting her go.

Delanie turned back to the kitchen, an eye on the clock. It was still early, she knew, but Don needed to eat. So did she. She rushed to start preparing a meal, hearing Aidan's voice speaking with Don. It couldn't be good if he was here this early.

Aidan walked towards the kitchen, following Don. He assessed Don as he did so. Don was still in rough shape. That worried him. It wasn't what he wanted to see. It would be difficult to protect him at any time but this made it so much worse. Aidan turned to Delanie, assessing her as well. He could see that she was shaken and worried as well even though she was trying hard to hide it from him. Sitting back after the meal had finished and they had spent some time in prayer, Don studied Aidan. He was here for a reason and he wanted to know why.

"Aidan? What can you tell us?" Don wrapped an arm around Delanie. "Where does the investigation stand?"

Aidan nodded before he reached for the folder that he had set to one side. His hand rested on it for a moment.

"We're finding information now that we had not been able to. People are approaching our officers with names and other information. George and I are working through it. There is a lot. Emma has been sending what she has found as well.

"The attack on you has been confirmed as directed towards the emergency services. The police force in fact. We are hearing rumours as to why and those we have to confirm. What I can tell you is that someone in town has a huge grudge towards us and is trying to harm our reputation in town. You were chosen because of your profile of being in security. They thought that we would be more concerned if you were hurt or harmed than if it had been an ordinary citizen. You know that isn't the truth."

"No, it's not. In fact, I would want it the other way. To investigate someone else rather than myself or my team. And those things that hung over from my team? That's involved."

"It is. That's been our feeling all along, hasn't it?" Aidan watched as Delanie nodded. "Delanie? Don has talked to you about that?"

"He has. And I have to agree. So, where do we go from here? How do we bring that person or persons out into the open so that you can arrest them?"

"This is where it becomes very dangerous for you both. We want you out in the open. Act as a newlywed couple would. That's what you are. You know the drill. Go for walks. Shop together. Go out for a meal. Go to church. See Don's family and friends."

Don was nodding as Aidan was speaking. That was what they had decided to do. They were tired of hiding from whoever it was. And if they stayed hidden, then the person would never come out into the open. Don was just afraid for Delanie. He was afraid that she would be hurt or killed and he just didn't know how to deal with that thought.

"God is our Defender, Aidan. He will protect us. He does not allow anything that He has not already known about. That is our confidence. He will avenge us if we are harmed. And I know that this is in His will for us." Delanie blinked for a moment, an attempt to control her emotions. "I have lived for years with the feeling that someone has been watching me. I don't know who but I would suspect that couple. They are likely sending information back to where I used to live. I refuse to live in fear."

Aidan studied her as she stopped speaking. Delanie had an iron streak in her that was coming out.

He smiled to himself. When she and Don had children, she would be like a mother bear protecting her cubs. She was just who Don needed in his life.

"Okay, so we do that. There will be officers who will be around you. There is a growing list of volunteers, Don. They want to do this for you just because of who you are and how you work with us. Not every security team does that."

"I always have. We need to work together to keep people safe." He frowned for a moment. "What huge festival is coming up?"

Aidan's eyes shot towards Don, shock on his face. He then nodded. This was it, wasn't it? It would be similar to what had happened in Riverville. It was up to them to solve this before it got that far.

"The festival in a month. The artist one. We draw people in from all over." Aidan's eyes slid closed. "And it's huge."

"It is. We need to solve this before then. So, how do we do it? How do we draw them out?"

Delanie was studying the men and then rose, returning with a calendar. She circled the festival date and then tapped each day prior to that.

"We do something every day, Don. We are out and about every single day. We are open that we are looking for whoever it is that is out there. Word will get to them and they will become careless in their rush to get to us."

"Delanie's right, Aidan. That's what we do. I'm just not sure I'm up to much for the next few days." Don rubbed at his face, feeling a headache starting.

"We do simple things for the next few days, Don. Go out for a meal. Shop. Go into some of the shops. Head for the library. I want books to read and don't have them. We replace what we need to. Jack has offered us this house until we can decide what we want to do." Her hand reached for Don's.

Don nodded, his eyes on Aidan. He agreed with Delanie. They needed to talk about their home but that was a conversation for another day. Today? They needed to start making plans and then reaching out to his team to finalize them. It was not an option for his team to be excluded. And he knew full well that Abe and his team and Richard and his team would be involved. It was what they did for one another.

Chapter 33

Two days later, Don walked through the downtown area. He was still sore and a bit unsteady on his feet but he knew that if he stayed inside, this would never be resolved. Delanie's hand was tight in his. Members of the police force were following them but he didn't acknowledge them. Some of his team were around them as well.

Delanie pulled Don to a stop at a store, staring through the window. The bakery was near closing for the day but she was through the door, heading for the counter. Don followed her, not sure what she was up to but willing to follow her.

Turning from the counter, Delanie's face was wreathed in smiles. Don grinned at her as he reached for the bags of buns and sweets that she had chosen. He dropped a kiss on her cheek bringing her hand to the spot and a smile to spread even wider on her face.

"Where to now, Don?" Delanie stood for a moment, her eyes searching for the men after them.

"We drop this back in your car and then we head to Ben's for a meal."

They walked back that way, Thomas and Paul following them.

"They're heading for a meal." Paul searched the area around them, knowing that someone was watching Don and Delanie.

"It would suspect Ben's." Thomas started walking that way, Don and Delanie ahead of them.

"It looks that way. Ben may have heard something." Paul reached for the door to the diner, pulling it open, and then heading for the kitchen. Thomas instead headed for a table where they would be able to have a meal and yet keep an eye on Don and Delanie.

Ben looked up from his desk work as Paul appeared and sat in a nearby chair. He studied the younger man, seeing the stress and strain that was on his face.

"Paul? What can I do for you?"

"I really don't know, Ben. Have you heard any scuttlebutt on the street about Don and Delanie?" Paul was hoping that he had and that it would solve the mystery that night.

Ben stared at him for a moment before he reached for an envelope. It had been dropped off on the front counter not that long ago. He had been handed it. It simply had Don's name on it.

"This. It was dropped on the counter about ten minutes ago. I hadn't had a chance to call Don yet."

Paul reached for it and tucked it into a pocket.

"Don and Delanie are here. I'll make sure that he gets it. Nothing else?"

Ben shook his head. It was strange. He was always hearing the scuttlebutt and passing it on to whoever it needed to go to. This time, he just wasn't hearing that and that puzzled and worried him.

———

Don rose at last from the booth. He was exhausted and knew that Delanie would be as well. He nodded at Paul and Thomas, walking past them to head for the door. Thomas stopped him by stepping into his way.

"Let me have your keys, Don. We'll drive you home." Thomas waited patiently with a hand out, taking the keys that Delanie finally handed him. "Wait here and I'll grab it."

Paul stood beside Delanie, assessing the couple. He could see them wearing out and wearing down. He frowned. This is what was wanted, he decided. Wear them down and then they are less alert. Paul would need to speak with Don about that.

Delanie turned the next morning from the front window. She felt unsafe but didn't know why. Don had headed for the office, having asked her to come with him. She had refused, accepting his hug and kiss before he headed for Caleb's truck.

Turning once more to the window, Delanie chewed at her lip. She needed to be in her office but had simply changed the voice mail message to one that stated that she was out of the office for a family emergency. She felt that she was letting the kids down but her mind was not in the right spot to do just that.

Frustrated, Delanie reached for her purse and car keys. This was ridiculous, she decided. She needed to continue her life and part of that was her work. She headed for the office, nodding at the officer who was waiting for her there. He followed her inside and walked through the building.

"It looks okay, Delanie." He grinned at her. "I'm here for the day. I'll be in the waiting room until you're ready to leave."

"Thank you. That does help." Delanie was soon engrossed in her work, saying a soft thank you as a mug of coffee appeared on her desk.

Rising four hours later, Delanie stretched and then stared down at her desk. She had managed to get caught up with the phone calls that were needed. Her clients' parents were very understanding. They all assured her that they were willing to work with her on what needed to be done.

Delanie walked through the office, searching for the police officer. A momentary bit of panic hit hurt until he appeared from the kitchen.

"You're still here!"

He grinned at her.

"I am. All done?"

"I am. I just need to clean up my mess." She frowned at him as he shook his head. "What?"

"It's done, Delanie. Now, let's get you home. I have an officer here to drive your car home." His face was grim as he said that.

"You have? You are? Okay, I guess that's how it works." Delanie waited patiently for the officer to search outside the door and then beckon for her to follow him.

Late that afternoon, Don appeared in the home office doorway, watching Delanie as she worked away.

He saw her jump in fear as she heard a noise and waited for her to look up.

"Don!" Delanie was on her feet, throwing herself at him. "I was so afraid that you were hurt again."

"No, I'm here. Delanie, we need to talk and talk tonight." Don simply held his bride tight in his arms. He was so afraid for her, given what they had discovered that day.

Chapter 34

"How was your day?" Don leaned back to stare down at Delanie.

Delanie shrugged. She wasn't sure what to say.

"It was okay. I was able to get caught up at the office. An officer was with me the whole time." Her head went down on his shoulder. "How was yours?"

"It was interesting, to say the least. The team that is in for training is great and eager to learn. Now, about our adventure? We've discovered something that we need to talk about. But that we can do later."

Delanie nodded, knowing that they did need to talk but she felt that they needed to pray more.

"We need to pray more than that, Don. We're coming up to where it gets very dangerous for us."

"You are correct, sweetheart." Don turned them from the office towards the living room. "Are you hungry right now?"

"No, I'm not. Are you?" She frowned at him when he shook his head. "We spend the time in prayer instead?"

"We will." Don drew her down to the couch, keeping an arm around her. "We need to do that, sweetheart."

An hour later, Don raised his head. They had spent the hour in prayer and then just waiting for the peace that only God can give to flow through them. They had reached that point.

Delanie refused to move from Don's arms. She was content and felt safe with him. Now, they just needed to solve their mystery.

"Don, where does the investigation stand? I haven't heard in a couple of days."

"About that. We're working through it but we would like it if you could come to the office tomorrow." Don watched the emotions flickering across her face.

"I can do that. But what can you tell me?"

"We are narrowing it down to a dozen people or so. They are high in the town politics. And that's why it's been difficult to determine who it is. They do have information about the emergency services that the ordinary person would not have."

Delanie nodded, her hair brushing against Don's chin.

"That's about what I figured. Now, how do we narrow it down enough to determine who it is?"

"We have a database that Mark set up and is working on. Our whiteboards are full on information. Richard and Abe are breaking themselves loose tomorrow and heading our way. Emma will be here as well. They want to help us work through what we have."

"I see. We are going to owe so much." She felt Don's head shaking in the negative.

———

"We're friends, Delanie. Richard and I have been friends since we were babies. Our parents were friends and lived next door to one another. Abe is a good friend, first because of our security teams and now because of what we have all faced. It has drawn us into a close bond that we don't have with others."

"I can see that. Support is important at times like this. I have been receiving calls from so many ladies that I can't keep track of them all."

"Write out their names and I'll tell you who they belong to." Don stretched out his legs, not wanting to move but knowing that at some point they would need to. He felt Delanie's head growing heavier on his shoulder and realized that she had dozed off. His head went down on hers as he began to petition God for her safety. It was not long before he slept as well.

The next morning, Delanie wandered around the conference room, eying the piles of paper on the table and then the whiteboards. She walked along the wall, stopping at each board to read what was on it. She was surprised at what information was there, including information about her family.

Don watched her before he turned away. He was due in the training facility and headed that way as much as he wanted to stay with Delanie. Mark nodded at him as he headed towards Delanie, handing over a cup of tea.

"Delanie? What do you need to know?" Mark grinned at her.

"This? How did you discover so much?" Delanie turned to him as he gave a soft laugh.

"We just start with a name and then keep expanding our searches. Emma has helped with that as has her team. A friend has set up a family tree for you and Don and Emma will bring that today." His hand went up. "Kat does this for us. She's married to one of Abe's team members."

"I see. Okay. Then walk me through what you know for certain. I am interested in what you have put down for my family. I never knew that about them."

"You didn't? They never talked about what they did?" Mark was not surprised at that. It had been discussed between the team and that was the consensus that they had come to.

"No, not in front of me. I never knew what their occupations were. I guess I lost interest when they treated me as they did."

"That would do it." Mark's hand drew out a chair and he gently shoved her to a seating position, taking her cup and placing it on the table beside her. "Okay. So your parents? They are not on the up and up, shall we say? We haven't totally proven that they are into crime but if they're not, they are close to it."

"I see. They worked blue-collar jobs but seemed to have money. I couldn't understand how they had the money that they did. I know that their jobs didn't pay that well."

"No, they don't. Emma's been able to confirm their occupations and wages. Now, this is what we do know about their friends." Mark continued to speak, rising to point at different names.

Delanie nodded as he spoke. She knew all the names but had not realized that they were friends with her parents. Her hand rose at one point to stop him.

"That last name? He's on the police services board or was when I lived there. Does he have a connection to here?"

Mark nodded. Delanie had pinpointed something in just a few moments that it had taken them hours to discover.

"He does, Delanie. Unfortunately, he does. We think that may be how he found out where you were. You disappeared and they found some link to here. He approached his contact here and they found you. You have been watched likely for years until now. They connected you with Don when you met on the trail. Since then, two parties have been after you."

Delanie paled at that thought. She was suddenly and deeply afraid. How did she do this? All she could do was beg God for His protection and defense.

Chapter 35

Abe and Richard shared a look with one another. It was now late afternoon and the two couples had arrived along with Doug and Darcy. Doug had been adamant that they needed to be there, given their history with a rogue law enforcement official. Abe had nodded, knowing that Doug was correct. He and Doug were cousins and shared a love for all things legal. They were both very worried about Don.

"Delanie?" Richard's voice brought her head up from the material that she was reading. "Talk with us."

Delanie shared a look with Richard and then Abe. She did need to discuss what she was reading. She didn't understand it at all.

"This? I don't understand it." She shoved it towards Abe whose hand landed on it to stop it. "Explain it to me."

Abe scanned through it and sighed. She had the most difficult part of the investigation in front of her. Now, he needed to sort it out and help her. Thomas had moved up to sit beside him.

"Thomas? What is this?" Abe pointed at the material.

"That? That's the connection between Delanie's town and here. We discovered that one of her father's friends is still on the police services board there. He is friends with one of the members from here. We think that they have known all along where Delanie has been and have been watching her." Thomas' face grew grim. "And that because of how she and Don met? That drew her into whatever they're going after Don about."

"That makes sense." Abe looked around as he heard more footsteps. Aidan, George, and Kaelen had appeared. "Kaelen flies, doesn't he?"

"He does. He's been back over the trails a number of times and can't figure it out."

"No? Then there can't be anything there." Richard was on his feet, approaching Kaelen. The two men were soon deep in conversation, moving away from the conference room as they did so.

Delanie watched them closely and then sighed. This was not how her day was to have been. She had had plans for that day that included just resting and then working on what she needed to for the kids. That had not happened. She rose and walked away from the men, heading for Don's office. She slumped into his chair, her eyes closing as she tried to control her tears. That didn't happen. Her head ended up buried in her folded arms on the desk top.

Emma had come to look for her, pausing as she saw Delanie sobbing. She knew only too well how that felt. She moved forward to sit in front of the desk, her head bowing as she prayed. Her prayer became audible.

Delanie heard the prayer and raised her head, blinking to clear her eyes. She stared at Emma before she sighed. She had wanted to be alone. Only that had not happened.

Emma's gaze was on Delanie, waiting for her to speak. If she didn't, Emma intended to simply sit with her.

"Emma? What would you do?" Delanie's voice was low and tear-filled.

"What would I do? I can tell you what I would do. I would fight and fight hard. I would face my parents and tell them exactly what I think of them. I would then turn to this town and be out there in the open as much as I could. I would put out word that I am looking for so and so and then hunt for him openly." Emma paused, her thoughts racing faster than her words. "And then I would just keep repeating what I was doing. I would involve the team and their ladies as well as Don's family. Richard's and Abe's teams are not going to sit back, you do know that? We've been through too much to walk away from Don or you."

"Thank you, Emma. This helps. We need to come up with a plan to do just this." Delanie was on her face, heading for the door only to find Don standing there with a warm wet cloth in his hand to wash away the traces of her tears. He then wrapped her into as tight a hug as he could. His prayer whispered in his ear.

The team turned to face Don as he walked to the head of the table, Delanie's hand tight in his. He stared down as her upturned face, seeing the same determination in her as he knew was in him.

"People? This is crunch time. Emma has challenged us to go on the offensive. I know that

<hr>

we've been talking about that but have kept it very low key. That changes as of now. We don't have a team in for the next week or so. Let's see what we can do to make this end by next week. Aidan? Are you on board?"

"We are, Don. We have some ideas but let's hear what your team and Richard and Abe come up with. They've had the experience in this, unfortunately, just as you have had. We've been on the investigative side and will remain there. But you will have protection as you are out and about. That will not change."

Don nodded before his head bowed and he began to pray. The prayer was taken up one by one by those around them. Don stated afterwards that he felt the presence of God in the room in a way that he never had before. Delanie stated that she had seen an angel in the corner at the back, just watching the couple in silence. Don had stared at her and nodded, knowing that it was entirely possible that an angel had been there.

The men bent to the task, ideas bouncing back and forth among them. Delanie stood and watched before she glanced at Emma and then the ladies from the team who had shown up. She pointed to the door and walked that way.

"They'll not stop for a meal unless we prepare it, will they?" Delanie shared a look with all of the ladies. "We need to do something about that."

"Okay. So we do a food run." Taran had her keys out. "Who's with me?" Payton and Cullea headed out with her, leaving the other four ladies to stare around.

"We can set up in the other board room. It's smaller but it will be enough for our meal." Delanie flipped on the light switch and moved into the room. "There is enough room for all of us."

"What about dishes and cutlery?" Emma moved in beside to help Delanie set up the room.

"We have a supply that is more than ample." McKala headed for the kitchen, Jincy with her.

Two hours later, Delanie appeared in the midst of the men, taking the paperwork from their hands and dropping it to the table. They looked at her in shock.

"We have a meal ready for us. Come now. We eat and then pray. You need a break." Delanie turned and walked away, leaving the men to stare at one another and then rise and follow her.

Chapter 36

The next day, Don paced the office as he waited for Delanie to appear. He had asked her out for a dress-up dinner and she had brightened up at that request. He was in a suit and tie and had a bouquet of roses for her.

Delanie paused for a moment, taking in Don as he stood waiting for her, a grin on her face. She moved quickly towards him and into his arms. She was content to be held but knew that they were still in danger. Tonight was part of the plans that they had come up with. Her roses were quickly placed in a vase.

Don walked Delanie towards a classy restaurant, one of the nicer ones in town. He was glad to have her with him but he still worried about her. And he knew that she was worried about him. They had spent many hours in prayer since the decision to go on the offensive.

Aidan looked around as he too entered the restaurant. He had chosen to be the one protecting Don and Delanie that night. He knew that other officers were inside and outside as well.

Their meal finished, Don and Delanie headed outside, knowing that this was a dangerous time for them. Aidan trailed after them, not watching them but watching the area around them. He was worried. Don had remembered nothing about what had happened to him just a few days ago. And his truck had not been found. It could be anywhere by now, Aidan acknowledged, or even taken to a scrap yard and destroyed.

A sudden squeal of tires caused Don's head to shoot around. He wrapped Delanie in his arms and threw himself sideways, rolling as he hit the pavement. He then covered her with his body, his weight holding her to the pavement despite her protest. Don stared in shock at the truck that sped away. His truck? His truck was just used to try and run him and Delanie down.

Don felt a hand slap on his back, holding him down. He knew it was one of the officers protecting him. He didn't realize that Mark, Joshua, Caleb, Thomas, and Paul had been there. It was Thomas' hand that slapped him and held him down.

Aidan ran towards his car, heading out after the truck. He didn't realize that it was Don's truck until the plate was run and the name came back on the air. His face paled at that thought of Don't truck used against him. He lost sight of the truck. Frustration set in before he headed back towards the restaurant. By this time, Don was on his feet, Delanie wrapped tight to his side. Thomas had finally allowed Don and Delanie to stand albeit surrounded by the team.

Aidan walked towards Don, assessing the couple. Don was angry and Delanie was as well. He sighed. This was not what they had expected.

"Don?" Aidan's voice cut through Don's anger.

"Aidan? That was my truck!" Don spit out the words.

"I know. I lost it. And I want to know who was driving it." Aidan's anger caused his words to have a bit to them.

Delanie looked around Don at him, a frown on her face. She had a thought that she needed to run by Don and that could not be done then.

At home, Delanie changed into casual clothes, distraught that their date night had been so disturbed. Don watched her as she made them coffee before he reached for a tin of sweets that Delanie had baked earlier that day.

Delanie curled up in one corner of the couch. Don had lit the gas fireplace and then sat on the couch facing her. He waited for Delanie to speak, knowing that if he did, his anger would spill out.

"Don? I think I know who it is." Delanie drew in a deep breath. She said a name, a name of a woman who was prominent in town and always seemed to be a big supporter of the emergency services.

Don thought through what he knew of the woman before he nodded. Delanie had confirmed an idea niggling at the edge of his mind.

"I think that you're right. She would be the perfect one to do this." Don's head tilted as he looked up, seeking answers from the heavens. "How do we prove this?"

Delanie spoke rapidly, her plan forming as she spoke. Don listened intently and then added his thoughts.

"Will this work?" Delanie was desperate to know that it would.

"I think it will. We'll talk to the team tomorrow and reach out to Richard and Abe. I think we need to leave Aidan and the police out of it for now. We need to call off our security when we're out. You know what that means."

"I do. We're putting ourselves out there and at risk. It's going to be hard to do this, Don." She blinked rapidly for a moment. "But we have to. God is using us to bring this person or persons to justice. We can't walk away. Who all has she hurt for all these years?"

"That's it, sweetheart. We don't know that. I'm not sure who all she would have hurt but I am sure that it's not going to be a very pretty picture."

"It never is." Delanie moved to curl up against Don, his arms tight around her and bringing comfort to both of them. "I love you, Don. I don't want you hurt again."

"I love you too, sweetheart. I don't want to see you hurt but it's a real possibility."

"I know. I talked to Darcy this morning about what happened to her. Doug almost lost her."

"He did." Don reached for his phone as it chimed. It was Abe.

"Abe?"

"Don? Are you two okay?"

Don could hear the worry in Abe's voice.

"We are. Who reached out to you?"

"Paul. He's drawing in our team and Richard's team tomorrow."

"Good. We need to meet. Delanie has come up with a name."

"And can you share?" Abe's question drew Emma's attention to him.

"I can." Don gave him the name and heard Emma's exclamation. "What did Emma say?"

"She had come across that name and was investigating it. She's not a very nice person."

"On the surface, she is. She supports the emergency services. That way, she knows what is going on with them."

"She would. Listen. I won't keep you. We'll see you in the morning."

Don set aside his phone, content for the moment just to hold the love of his life. He just was scared that he would lose her. Don realized that he was doing God's work but couldn't help himself. That was the humanness in him.

Chapter 37

The three teams stared at Don the next morning as he described what Delanie had suggested and who. They shared looks with one another before Don's team began to nod. Delanie had pegged the person, that much they knew. Now, they had to prove it.

"Don, what are your plans?" Richard spoke up, his eyes on his friend.

"That we need to refine. We still plan on being out and about as much as we can. We're not letting Aidan in on this until we have confirmation. We don't want to scare her away."

Richard wasn't sure if that was the right move but it was Don's decision, his and Delanie's. He may have made the same decision, he was aware, if that had been him.

"What else?" Abe spoke up.

"We could go to the media but we don't want to at this point. That is something that we are keeping in mind." Delanie spoke up from where she sat near Abe. "We could picket in front of her place with huge signs that call her out. I want to do that. Don isn't sure if that's a good idea." She smirked at Don as he grinned at her.

"That would certainly bring attention to her. How long do you plan to keep doing this?" Micah from Abe's team spoke up.

"We think a week. Scuttlebutt on the street is that she is planning something soon. We want to force her hand before that happens." Don knew that it was a tight timeline for them. "We need to consider plans that we can ramp up every day."

"And we will." Murphy from Abe's team had already been thinking through what needed to be done. "Abe, you and Emma did something like this."

"We did. We didn't want to but we had to. It did help. I'm not sure if that will with Don and Delanie." Abe and Emma shared a look before Emma turned back to her laptop and her investigations.

Delanie rose and stretched, needing to move around. She turned to study Don, seeing that he was deep in discussion with his team. She leaned back against a wall, not sure what to say or what to think.

Ian rose and approached her. He was one of Abe's team and was deeply worried about Don and Delanie.

"Delanie? What are your thoughts?"

Delanie shrugged, not sure any more what to think.

"I'm not sure, Ian. And before you say anything, we're not ready to be flown anywhere to hide. I know that's what you always offer the ladies. Besides Kaelen has already offered that." She smirked at him as he grinned at her. "My thoughts? We need to do this. I'm just not sure that we're making the right choice. We have to do this. We have to bring her out into the open. I just worry that Don will be hurt or that some innocent bystander will be."

"We know that, Delanie. We know the concerns that you have. And we want to help you with those." Ian's hand drew her from the room and to the reception area. He shoved her down into a chair, left and then returned quickly with a bottle of water that he handed her.

"Ian, would you do this?"

"I would. Lydia and I went through some hard stuff as did all our team. We want to help you both. What can we do?"

Delanie shrugged, not sure what to say.

"What do we do?" Delanie looked up as Don sat beside her, his hand reaching for hers. "Don?"

"It's okay, sweetheart. We'll pray our way through this. The fellows have come up with some suggestions that we need to go over."

"We do? Okay. But not right now. Ian was going to fly us away somewhere until this was all over." She smirked at Ian as he laughed at her.

"He was, was he?" Don grinned at her. "Now, what do we do? We have plans to put into place. And places to be found."

"I know. I wish this was all over." Delanie frowned at the floor, not sure what she was to think.

"It will be soon, sweetheart. We're hearing rumbles from the street that she is getting desperate for something that we don't know about."

———

"I heard that from Ben." Delanie stared at Don, realizing what he was saying. "So, if we ramp up the efforts against her in the next few days, she'll make a mistake and they'll be able to find and arrest her."

"I know that, sweetheart. And Ben is correct. There are rumblings on the street involving her. We need to figure out how to do this without getting either one of us killed. And she will do that, I have no doubt."

Delanie shuddered at the thought of that but she knew that Don was correct. Their plan would go into effect on the morrow. She just prayed that their tactics would be effective.

The teams from out of town finally left, not sure that Don and Delanie would be safe. They planned to be around when they could but that might not happen in time.

Don didn't sleep that night. He spent the night in prayer. He could hear Delanie moving quietly around the house, knowing that she was not sleeping either. Don rose at last from his office chair and went to find her. She was standing at the front window, the drapes open with no lights on. She was just staring out into the night.

"Sweetheart? Can't sleep?" Don knew that she likely shared his thoughts and worries.

Delanie shook her head. She had known that Don was in his office but had not wanted to disturb him.

"No, I can't. I'm worried, Don, that we are making the wrong decision. We're going on the offensive against someone who is dangerous."

"She is but our God is much bigger and stronger than she is. We'll stand with His protection and defense." Don prayed for her once more, wrapping her into a tight hug. He didn't want to lose her but that was a real possibility.

Chapter 38

Don and Delanie began to put their plans into play the very next morning. They walked through the downtown area, knowing that they were putting themselves at risk. They were willing to do that. They were afraid for what the woman might do in the next few weeks and felt that putting their own lives on the line may well save many others. The investigation that they had started on her led them to believe that she had killed before and would not hesitate to do that again.

The woman stood in her office at the window that overlooked the downtown street. She glared down at Don and Delanie, knowing that they could not see her. Hate continued to grow in her heart towards them and by extension to the emergency services just because of Don's connection to them. She turned as a tap came to her office door and her face was wreathed in smiles even as her heart continue to burn with hate.

The chairman of the police services board stood there, an envelope in his hand. He stared at the woman, wondering how she had hidden so much. An investigation that was separate from what Don and his team were involved in had proven that she was deeply into crime and had been hiding it all too well.

"This is for you." The man, in his fifties, stood in front of her, a stern look on his face. "You are relieved of any duties with the emergency services boards. Our lawyer will be in touch." He dropped the envelope to her desk and walked away, the door closely softly behind him.

She glared at the door, anger burning within her. She would take them all down, she decided, and would begin with Don and his team. That had been her goal. This paperwork? She flicked a finger at it. It didn't mean anything. Not a chance. She strode from her office, the temporary secretary looking up in fear. The woman had not been able to keep a secretary for years. This young woman watched her leave and then just reached to gather her belongings. She would not stay there. There was evil in that place and she was deeply afraid.

Don could feel the evil growing closer to them. He shuddered for a moment as he looked around. He frowned at Delanie as she looked up at him, a puzzled look on her face. She could feel the evil around them as well.

"Don? Who's out there?" Delanie's voice was low and shaky.

"She's out here, sweetheart. Somewhere. We'll just keep doing what we're doing." Don pulled her forward, in and out of stores and shops. They ended up at a small cafe where they chose a table outside. Don disappeared into the cafe and returned with a tray of food for them.

They ate slowly, conversation low between them. They kept watch on the passersby, knowing that Don's team was there somewhere. They just couldn't see them.

The woman watched from the shadows. She had found men who would move in on the couple and bring them to her. She had a place ready for them. They would stay hidden away while she put her other plans into place. Once the devastation had happened, Don and Delanie would reappear and be blamed for everything. She cackled to herself at the thought of that.

Don tidied away the garbage from their meal and returned the tray to the cafe. He was smiling as he approached Delanie and walked away with her, in the opposite direction from the woman. Her face grew ugly with her rage before she ordered the hirelings to follow them and bring them to her.

The men moved after Don and Delanie, not seeing Don's team move in on them and prevent them from moving forward. The men were quickly taken into custody by Aidan and his team.

Aidan stared at the team, a frown on his face.

"Fellows? You're up to something."

Mark shared a look with his team mates.

"We're just doing what they said they would do. They're out and about. We're providing security for them."

Aidan drew a deep breath. They were correct. Don and Delanie had planned to do that. He just felt that there was more to it than what he was being told.

Don pulled out his phone as it chimed. He showed the text message to Delanie who nodded. The team may have stopped two men but there would be more out there. They just didn't know who they would be.

His steps halting, Don's hand tightened on Delanie's. This was it, he thought, staring at the gun pointing at Delanie's head. They had no choice but to follow the man, with two men dropping in behind them.

The couple was led to a nearby building and forced up the stairs to the third floor. Delanie's purse was pulled from her shoulder despite her protest and Don's phone was yanked form his belt. The door was slammed behind the men and locked.

Delanie fled into Don's arms, shudders shaking her as she tried to control her sobs. Her emotions were raw and this was just the final push to sending them over the edge. Don held her, frustrated that they had been taken. He wasn't sure that the team even knew that they had disappeared.

Thomas searched for Don and Delanie, not seeing them. He grew afraid for them. Paul paused beside him.

"Do you see them?" He too was searching the area.

"No. They've disappeared. This is what we wanted to avoid and was afraid would happen."

"It is. Now we need to find them. I don't think they were taken out of the area." Paul turned as the other three men moved in. "They're been taken, guys."

Grim looks covered the men's faces. Aidan approached them carefully, not liking the looks on their faces.

"Fellows?"

"Don and Delanie are gone, Aidan. I think those two men were a plant and she had someone else waiting for them. They had to have threatened Delanie. Don would not have gone otherwise." Mark was frustrated at that.

Aidan nodded, reaching for his phone. The areas would be searched and security video pulled from the stores. He wasn't sure that they would be of any help.

Chapter 39

To say Aidan was worried and frustrated would be an understatement. He was deeply worried about Don and Delanie. He had not expected to have them disappear from a street as busy as it was with pedestrians.

Mark stood with his arm around McKala, facing the other men and their ladies. They had gathered at the office building and in the conference room. They were having trouble believing that Don and Delanie had just disappeared even though they knew that was what had happened.

"What buildings are around there, Mark?" Joshua sat at a computer, Jincy close to him. "Does she own any of them?"

"I have no idea. Samuel would be a good one to tell us or Emma." Caleb had reached out to a friend who was a title searcher and also to Emma. He had had to leave a voice mail for Emma.

"They would be. They'll work it as a priority." Paul rubbed at his face, his eyes on Payton. "Payton? You have a thought."

"I do. We would expect them to be taken out of the area overnight. I don't think that they will. She'll want us looking somewhere else for them. I would say that they are in a building within a block of the restaurant." She looked around and saw the nods of agreement.

"I think that Payton's right." Thomas reached for the tray of mugs that Taran appeared with. "Here. It's going to be a long night. Let's spend some time in prayer and then start our search."

Early morning found the men rubbing at their eyes, tired and worried. They were finding the trail of the woman and it was just what they had expected to find. Abe and Richard had shown up around midnight, joining in the search.

The men looked up as they sensed movement in the room and then were on their feet. The ladies had been busy preparing a meal for them. Once they had eaten, they gathered to pray, knowing that God was in control and would defend their friends.

Abe turned from the whiteboards, assessing the men. He could tell that they were worried but were also determined to find Don and Delanie and to do that within the next day or so. The information that they had been finding only confirmed the depths of depravity that the woman would sink to.

Caleb was on his feet, heading for a whiteboard. He wiped away names and wrote only one name back on it. The men were on their feet, staring at the name.

"Caleb?" Thomas spoke for the group.

"He's involved." Caleb turned back to his team. He held up a paper. "He's her brother. And he is deep into crime. He has hidden it so well."

"He has." Richard knew the name and was afraid for his friends. "And he is involved with the emergency services."

Joshua sorted through his paperwork that he had been randomly printed and held up a sheaf of paper.

"This goes with that." He walked towards Caleb. "He has a wide empire of crime. How did we not know that?"

"They hide and hide well, Joshua." Abe reached for the paperwork, scanned it and then passed it on.

The men read the reports and then stared at one another. Jincy reached to take them and read the words, the ladies gathered around them.

"Okay. So, he has a building downtown? That's where they'll be. We need to confirm that before we pass it on to Aidan." Taran looked up, surprised to find Aidan standing in front of her. "Aidan?"

"You have been busy, haven't you? And I was told to come and work with you. Toryn sent me." Aidan gently took the paperwork before he read it, heading to make a copy of it.

The group watched him, seeing the grim look on his face and then looked at one another. It was good, they all decided, that Aidan had shown up. But it was also not what they had wanted.

"He has another property, Aidan." Paul looked up from his phone. "Samuel's confirmed that he has a large estate just outside of town." He looked around. "I say that we have Kaelen fly over it and confirm if there is any activity at all."

Aidan had turned as Paul spoke, his mind racing at the possibilities. He was out of the room and heading for Kaelen. Somehow, he was not surprised to see that man walking towards him.

"Kaelen?" Aidan's voice stopped him and he looked up at the officer.

"Aidan? You're on a mission." Kaelen gave a grim smile.

"I am. I was looking for you. I need you to fly over a property for me. I'm requesting it in an official capacity." Aidan's hand on Kaelen's shoulder turned him back to his truck. "Let's head out. By the time that you're ready to fly, it will be light enough."

Kaelen shrugged, a wave directed at Thomas who stood just outside of the office building. Thomas nodded. This is what they needed, he knew. He just wanted to be the one to go with them. He stood for a moment before he ran after them. Aidan looked around and then nodded. It was okay, he decided, that Thomas come with them.

The helicopter flew a few passes over the property as Aidan and Thomas watched carefully. Thomas had taken the camera that Kaelen handed him and took what photos Aidan had asked for. He was not prepared to just hand them over. He wanted copies of them as well. He watched Aidan carefully as he forwarded the photos to his phone.

The four other team members turned as Thomas flew into the room, his phone held in the air. They were on their feet, approaching him, questioning where he had been.

———

"Thomas? Where were you?" Joshua reached for the phone. "What's this?"

"Aidan had Kaelen fly over a property. I tagged along. These are the photos that he had me take. I copied them to my phone." He bit at his lip for a moment. "I'm not sure that I should have, but he didn't say that it was an official police investigation. And it was Kaelen's camera that was used. Kaelen saw me doing this."

Joshua nodded, knowing how conflicted Thomas would be. He took Thomas' phone and transferred the photos to his computer. He then began to scroll through them, the other four men gathered around him. Shock covered their faces as Joshua paused at a photo.

"Is that who I think it is?" Caleb pointed at the man whose face was upturned to the sky.

"It is. He's involved?" Mark shook his head. "And that makes it even worse."

Chapter 40

The five men stared at one another before they were on their feet and headed for a large map on the wall. They stood around, deep in conversation before they had come to a consensus.

The ladies looked up as the men found them, frowning at them before they were on their feet. They were not sure what their fellows were put to but they were certain that there was a plan in place.

Mark turned from his back door that night, finding McKala waiting for him.

"Mark? What was that all about this afternoon?"

"Aidan wanted to fly over a property. There was no way that one of us was not going. He just let it. Those photos? I took them for him and for us. I think that he knew that I had a copy. He didn't say that I couldn't have them." Mark wrapped McKala in his arms. "I'm sorry, love."

"For what?" McKala frowned up at him.

"For putting you through this again. This is not what we need, none of us."

"No, it's not but it is what God has allowed." McKala hugged her husband tighter. "What did you discover on those photos?"

"A man who should not be out there. He is deep into crime as far as we can tell." Mark sighed. "We need to find him in town and then follow him. He has to be involved."

"We will. We'll pray him into custody." McKala walked away, worried about their friends.

The next morning, the team gathered once more in the conference room. They spent the first hour in prayer and then dived into their investigations. Paul sat back at last, his eyes on the whiteboards. On his feet, he walked along the wall, studying the information there.

"Paul? What are your thoughts?" Caleb leaned against the wall, his arms folded across his chest.

"I think that we are on the right track. There is just that one piece of information that we need to find."

"There is. I just wish I knew what it was." Paul paced, his hands jammed into his jeans' pocket.

"Me too." Mark had approached as well, his hand rubbing at the back of his neck. "What are we missing?"

Joshua looked up from where he was reading the material that he had just printed.

"This. The man? He has arrest warrants out for him in other jurisdictions. Aidan just let me know that. He's heading off to find the man with arrest and search warrants."

"This is going to be difficult." Paul turned to lean against the wall and face the other four. "We need to find Don and Delanie. How do we do that?"

Mark was nodding, his eyes narrowed. Then he snapped his fingers.

"I know how to do that." Mark spoke rapidly with the other men adding their thoughts.

"We're agreed?" Joshua looked around the group.

"We are." Caleb was nodding, reaching for his phone. "Let me send off a message to Abe and Richard." He pocketed his phone when he was done. "Let's get our flyers printed and then head for the downtown area." He grinned suddenly. "I think someone already knows where they are and is just waiting for us to approach them."

The other men laughed, the levity greatly needed. Flyers in hand, they headed for the downtown area. Ben stared at Joshua for a moment as he handed over a stack of flyers.

"You're saying that you want these handed out?" Ben studied the photos of Don and Delanie that were pictured on the flyer.

"If you would. We need to find them." Joshua hesitated for a moment. "You have not heard anything?"

"Not a word. And I should." Ben stared at Joshua. "That tells me that someone who is very dangerous has them. The people who live on the streets are afraid and that means that they wouldn't tell me."

"That's too true. If you hear anything, please call us." Joshua walked away, his eyes on the youth who was hanging around a bench nearby. He walked over there and sat, keeping his eyes off the youth. He waited patiently, knowing that the youth would speak when he felt safe.

"I know where they are." The youth kept his head down and his eyes fixed on the ground. "They're in the three-story building with the bookstore. On the top floor. We're going in tonight to get them." The youth hand rested on the bench near Joshua with the youth not asking for anything but taking gratefully the folded bill that Joshua push towards him.

Joshua watched him walk away and waited, his eyes on the crowds around him. He didn't feel watched but didn't think that he was on his own. He picked up his stack of flyers and continued on the route that he had chosen,

Back in the office building, the men were tired and worried. They were frustrated as well. They tried to pray but didn't know that it was helping. They were that discouraged.

Gideon walked in at that point, drawn to the building at God's insistence. He stared at the men and then just prayed for them.

"Okay, fellows. What can I do to help?"

The men shared a look before they turned back to Gideon. Words spewed forth from them in a rush. Gideon nodded. He would help without question.

Gideon walked into the downtown area late that night. He stopped in the shadows of a building, carefully watching the building where they were thought the couple was hidden. An hour passed before he saw dark forms moving in and heading for a door at the side of the building. Gideon moved slightly so that he could watch that door. He was also listening for any sound that might come from there.

Five minutes later, Gideon watched as the forms rushed from the building and towards him. He was soon part of the crowd as it almost ran towards where he had parked. His key fob was out as he clicked it to unlock the car door. Gideon was behind the wheel as he heard the soft clicking of the back doors. The crowd rushed away as he watched before he started the car and drove away. He heard soft motion in the back seat but didn't look around.

Gideon drove directly into his garage and then turned off the car. He shifted slightly to stare at the closed garage door before he spoke.

"Don? Delanie? We're in my garage. We can get into the house from here. Let's get you two inside."

Don was out of the car, pulling Delanie towards the door. They were inside in no time, turning to stare in shock at Gideon. Gideon stared back before he grinned.

"You two are safe. Let me let the fellows know. We'll connect you in the morning."

Delanie continued to stare at him, not sure what had just happened. All she knew was that she and Don were free.

Chapter 41

Delanie rolled over in bed the next morning, staring at the painted wall in front of her. She could feel Don's arm around her and felt safe again. She just wasn't sure where she was. On her feet, Delanie walked slowly through the house, looking for whoever it was that owned it.

She jumped as she heard a throat clearing, spinning to stare at whoever it was who had done that. Gideon stood behind her grinning.

"Delanie? You're on your feet? And hungry no doubt." He pointed behind him towards the kitchen. "Come on and eat. And someone dropped off some clean clothes for both of you."

"Thank you, Gideon. We appreciate that. It's been a rough day or so. Who were those people last night?" Delanie took the plate of food handed to her with a word of thanks before she sat and asked a blessing over it.

"People from the street. They were watching you when you were taken but weren't sure if you had gone willingly." He grinned as she snorted. "The fellows were handing out flyers yesterday and Joshua was approached by someone. He met with the team to come up with a plan. God told me that I had to be there to help. And help I did. I could move in and out without causing too much of a stir. It's what I do."

"I know. And thank you. You put your life at risk for us." Delanie studied him, worried about him now.

Gideon shrugged, knowing that she was correct but that he would gladly do it for anyone. It was how he felt that he was the hands and feet for Christ on earth.

"Now, what do we do with you two? They're going to be looking for you at the office and your home and at the homes of Don's parents, sister, and the team."

"I know." Delanie chewed at her toast, not tasting the sweetness and tartness combined of the grape jelly on it. "We have to come up with something."

"And we will." Don's arm was around her as he dropped a kiss on her temple. We'll figure it out, sweetheart."

"I know. I just worry about who is after us." Delanie leaned against him, finding comfort in his touch.

"We know who it is." Don's phone landed on the desk. "Mark has been in touch. Aidan has been working on search warrants and arrest warrants. He wants us to stay hidden for a couple of days." He looked over at Gideon and saw him nodding. "Gideon's okay with us staying here for a couple of days."

"I am. Take this time to spend it in prayer and Bible study. Take the time of intercessory prayer for the police and your friends and the emergency services. I'll be in and out."

Delanie debated about leaving and then shrugged. She turned to Don to find him watching her, a slight smile on his face. He was expecting her to say no and that they had to leave. She smirked at him.

"Thank you, Gideon. That would be lovely as long as you let me do the cooking." She smirked at Don as he brought out into laughter, Gideon joining in.

"Got me there, sweetheart." Don's hand rubbed at his mug. "Gideon, we'll need a go-between for us."

"And I can do that. I'm in and out and around town all the time. Your team can leave whatever they need to with Ben. I'm in there every afternoon for coffee. It's where I meet the people of the street who need me." Gideon was on his feet. "Hand over a list of what you need and I'll make sure that you get it." With their lists tucked into a pocket, Gideon walked away to the garage and then drove off.

Delanie stared at Don finding him returning her look. She frowned, not sure what they were to do to solve their mystery.

"Don? How do we solve this? Do you know the men who took us captive?"

Don was nodding as he listened to her.

"Unfortunately, I do. They work for the woman and also a man who is related to her. Rumour says that it is her brother but I don't think so."

"How do we research them? We don't have a computer."

Don grinned as he rose and then cleared away their dishes, Delanie's hands there to help him.

"We do. Paul sent on my laptop and I know that we can connect to Gideon's Wifi. I've done it before and he won't care."

"Okay. Let me see if I can find any paper and pens."

"Try his office. He has lots of pens and has paper near the printed." Don was working at starting up his laptop. He paused for a moment as Delanie sat back beside him, his eyes on her. "I love you, Delanie. You've been a great companion through all this. I would not have wanted to walk through it with anyone else."

Delanie's face softened as she listened to his words. She reached to hug him, her own words of love whispered in his ears.

"Now what?" Delanie shifted her chair closer to him to watch him work through his logins. "What is this?" She pointed to a picture that was waiting for him in his secure email.

"This man? He's the one who apparently owns the building where we were held." Don pointed at the email that Thomas had sent him. "And he says that Aidan, Kaelen, and he searched from the sky for another property. And they found it."

Delanie leaned her head against Don's shoulder. She yawned, suddenly exhausted.

———

"So, the guys are working this. And I am sure that the ladies are as well." She raised her head. "Can we do a conference call or something with them?"

"We can do that. Joshua has asked for that in about an hour. Abe and Richard want to be in on it." He dropped another kiss on her cheek. "It's getting there, sweetheart. We're finding the information that they need. And we will bring them down before they are able to harm any of the emergency services. I don't want to see what happened with Doug and Darcy and all the deaths and destruction that happened to the services in the area."

"I don't either. Darcy told me about it. Can we stop them in time? Do we need to go back out on the streets?"

"We may have to, sweetheart. But this time our guards will be a lot closer than they were." Don continued to read the material that the men had forwarded. His face grew grimmer as he did so. He heard Delanie's sharp intake of breath and turned to her. Her face had whitened.

"Delanie?"

"That man? He's a friend of Dad's from grade school. How did we not know that?"

Chapter 42

Don's team settled into their seats in the conference room, their ladies beside them. Abe and Richard had appeared, ready to help finalize any plans. They had just not been told that Don and Delanie were free.

"Don?" Caleb's voice echoed from Don's phone. "We're all here. First, are you and Delanie okay?"

"We're fine, Caleb, fellows, ladies. They did not harm us. We were simply locked into an empty loft in the building and left there. There was food and water left as well. It looks as if they planned to keep us there for a while."

"That's what we're being told." Paul spoke up at that point. "We have us all here, the ladies too. Richard and Abe as well. What can you tell us?"

"Not a lot. The men walked up to us and forced us up the stairs. I wasn't able to get much of a look at them because of their hoodies and sunglasses." Don turned as he heard a sound from Delanie. "Delanie?"

"They all had the same tattoo on the back of their right hands. It was a black square with a bee in the centre. I found it strange."

Richard and Abe shared a look. They had heard of a gang working the area for someone who was involved with the emergency services. Delanie had just confirmed it.

Mark looked up at that, a frown on his face. He shuffled through his paperwork, pulling up a paper.

"We came across that, Delanie. We just didn't know how the gang was connected to all this. Now we know. That makes it much more dangerous for you, Delanie. You do know that?"

Delanie's head dropped for a moment as she wiped at the tears on her face. She was overwrought, exhausted, and worried. Fear was sitting in her heart and she wanted that to be gone.

"I'm sorry, Mark. I didn't want this."

"We know that, Delanie. We do know that this is stressing both of you. I've sent on that information to Aidan and he will work through it. Now, how do we do this? We will likely need to put you two out on the street again."

"We realize that, Abe." Don's mind was whirling as he tried to come up with a plan that didn't put them in extreme danger. "What are your suggestions?"

"We put you out there tomorrow. They'll be looking for you since you disappeared. We stay close around you and have you both wired for sound. We will also rig up cameras of some kind. Joseph and Micah wanted to work on that with Don's team."

"That sounds like a plan. Okay. We'll plan on this for tomorrow. Now, can we pray, fellows, ladies? We need that." Don's head was bowed as he heard the prayers of his friends. God was there, he knew, protecting and defending them. Don also knew that sometimes bad things happened that were in God's will. He prayed for safety for his bride.

The next afternoon, Don and Delanie walked back through the downtown area. They could sense the evil moving in on them. The people who inhabited the streets watched the couple and then turned to watch the people around them. Don's team hovered close to them, their own attention not on the couple but on the people around them as well. The whole team was aware that this was a dangerous time for Don and Delanie,

Delanie felt Don's hand tighten on hers and she glanced up at him. He looked down at him and smiled. She sighed. She didn't want anything to happen to Don but she knew that it was a real possibility.

Don looked up before his steps slowed and then stopped. Delanie frowned as she looked up at Don. She could not understand why he had halted his steps. Her own gaze went ahead as she continued to frown. She had no idea who the woman was who stood in their way.

"Alice Grabell! I wondered when you would reappear." Don's loud call drew the attention of those around him. He could see his team moving in closer as they too saw the woman.

"Devlin! Of course I'm here. You are the reason why." Alice Grabell's face contorted with her rage.

"No, I don't think so." Don looked around, knowing that his team had their backs to the couple and were watching as well. "Where's Fred Grabell? We know that he is involved. And we know why."

———

"You know nothing. You are the reason why." Alice moved towards them, not seeing Abe and Richard flanking her.

Don nodded at the two men, knowing that they were ready to react if she made the slightest move towards them. Abe and Richard kept their eyes on Alice, knowing that others were around that would watch their backs.

Aidan had been at Ben's for a meal and stood watching the activity in front of him. He frowned as well as he recognized the woman. Moving closer to the activity, Aidan beckoned to the three officers that had been with him. They moved in as well to flank the group. Alice Grabell was not getting away, not this time. Aidan had an arrest warrant for her in his pocket, just by chance. He snorted. It was not by chance. God had prepared that for him and brought him there at the right time to arrest her.

Don shook his head, glancing around briefly. He wanted to get Delanie out of there but there was not going to be a chance for him to do that. He prayed for safety for his bride, knowing that it could go bad very quickly. Delanie moved as close to Don as she could, fear rising in her. This was it, she decided. Here, at that very moment, they lived or died.

Alice continued to walk towards them, hatred on her face. She wanted Don just because he was well known in town and well loved by the people. She didn't understand that it was because of who he was and not because of what he had.

———

"You're both coming with me." She reached out a claw-like hand to grab at Delanie. She jumped as she felt hands on her arms and began to struggle. Alice was unable to escape the hands no matter how much she struggled. She could also not escape the handcuffs that clicked around her wrists.

Don wrapped Delanie into his arms as he watched Alice led away. He turned his head slightly as Aidan approached. He knew that his team was still alert. They would be that way until Don and Delanie were out of the area. Richard and Abe had moved to stand in front of them.

"Aidan?" Don's voice was tired, exhaustion evident in how he slumped slightly.

"Don? You two are okay?" Aidan studied the two of them before he nodded. "We'll talk and soon." He walked away, knowing that he had to find Fred Grabell next and he knew exactly where he was.

"You okay?" Abe's voice was low even as he kept watch around his friends.

Chapter 43

A few days later, Aidan stepped into David's home, knowing that everyone had gathered there. He could hear happy conversation and laughter from the group and smiled. This time that he arrived here? It was with good news. Don and Delanie's adventure, this one at least, was over and he was so happy about it. God had protected his friends in ways that they had not even been aware of.

Don stood up from the couch when Aidan appeared, reaching out to hug his friend. Delanie rose as well to hug Aidan. She had not known him before this all began but she considered him a good friend now.

A meal was shared before David stood, waiting for silence to fill the room.

"Thank you all for how you worked to protect Don and Delanie. I know it's your job but you went well beyond that just because of your friendship. Abe. Richard. Your teams worked as well. We, as a family, cannot thank you enough. Let's spend some time in prayer before Aidan speaks. I for one am curious as to the whys of this." David sat back down, his hand reaching for Deree's.

They all could feel the presence of God in the room when the time of prayer had finished. Aidan sat with his head bowed for a few moments, his thoughts muddled. This was not him. He always thought clearly and concisely but this case had been different for him. It had involved crime in a province and also in a territory. That had led to other police forces becoming part of the investigation that had just continued to spread.

"Don. Delanie." Aidan paused his words, studying his friends. He nodded to himself. This couple was deeply in love and was not afraid to show it. God had protected them and defended them against foes that they didn't even know about. "You were well protected and defended by God. The deeper that we got into the investigation, the clearer it became that you were targeted, Don, simply because you are involved in security. They planned to set you up somehow to be used against the emergency services."

"How?" Mark spoke for the team.

"You know, those two have never really said. They're too busy blaming each other for their being arrested. We are still digging into their background and finding more and more information against them. Fred Grabell had a grudge against the police force going back to his brother. His brother died in an accident. It was investigated and determined to be that. He felt that the police had botched the investigation and that his brother had been murdered. Over the years, this had just festered in his mind like an abscess and it was ready to explode. Even though he was involved in boards and whatnot, he was not really liked. We're finding that he bought his way onto them. The same for Alice. She felt the same way about her cousin's death. She was not as obvious as Fred in her life of crime even though people always suspected her. The evidence was too well hidden."

———

"Until now." Delanie leaned her head against Don's shoulder. "Until now. And how do my parents fit in?"

"I'm sorry, Delanie. You were correct in your supposition. They were involved in crime up there. One of Fred's henchmen was a third cousin of your father's. He moved here at the same time as you did. He was sent to watch you and to keep your activities reported to your parents. They have been arrested but refuse to say why. He never knew. He became part of the group around Fred. The men who were on the trail that day? They were Fred's employees. Everything you went through was orchestrated by him. He fed enough information to Alice to make her think that it was all her plans but they weren't."

Don was nodding. This was the conclusion that he and Delanie had arrived at. But something still puzzled them.

"Aidan? There were always things that held over the other fellows' adventures. Joshua and Jincy for example. We never knew why they were forced to marry."

Aidan nodded once more. The arrests of Fred and Alice had explained all that.

"Fred and Alice were behind everything that your team went through that was unexplained. They hoped to chase you out of security, Don. They just didn't know your character and that of your team and friends."

Aidan walked away at last, exhausted and ready for that vacation he was to take. Toryn and Lyle had told him that he was not to come back to the office for three weeks. And that he was to please stay out of trouble. He had grinned and promised that he would do his best.

That evening, Don went looking for Delanie. He found her curled up in a chair in the room that he used as an office. He simply swept her into his arms and sat back down, content and happy with his life.

"Okay, sweetheart?" Don dropped a kiss on her cheek.

"I am. It saddens me to hear about my parents but I think that I always knew that. Now, what about you, my love?"

"I am. I have the life that I always wanted. I have the love of my life in my arms. And we are off on a new adventure called life." He kissed her, leaning back to look at her. "You're okay with all this?"

Delanie shrugged, still not sure about what all had happened. It would take days for her to process and process it she would.

"I'm okay. It will take time. I love you, Don. I am glad that God chose you to be my defender."

Don's arms tightened around her. He was exhausted as he knew that everyone around them was. Their adventure was over. He just prayed for whoever it would be next of their friends that faced danger. And that would happen. He had no doubt about that.

Two years later, Don stood on the back deck of their house, watching the group that had gathered. His team was there along with their ladies and the little ones that had joined the growing family. Richard and his team and their littles ones were there as were Abe, his team, and their littles one. He and Delanie had arranged a picnic for all of their friends that could make it. Others of their friends and the families of those friends mingled as well. Ben had catered the meal for them, glad to do that. He had waved away any offer for Don to repay him.

Don glanced down at the little one he held. His daughter was a month old and the image of her mother. Little Eden slept against his chest. He was in love with his daughter and it showed. He looked around as he felt a hand on his shoulder.

Richard stood beside his life-long friend, a smile on his face. He and Raleigh had welcomed their own son six months previously and felt that their family was now what it should be.

"Don? It's been a long struggle in some ways for us."

"It has been, Richard. When we were young and talked about what we wanted to do, we both knew that we wanted to help people. I just didn't expect to have happen what did to both of us." His hand rubbed at his daughter's back as she stirred slightly.

———

"No, it wasn't what we planned but it was what God had planned for us. He was our Protector and Defender through it all. I am glad that we both survived."

"As am I." Don turned as he heard steps beside him and reached to kiss Delanie before he touched the little boy that she held. They had had twins, not what they had ever dreamed of having. "Okay, sweetheart?"

"I am." Delanie grinned past him as she held little Ennis. "Thank you, Richard, for being who you are and the friend that we need."

That evening, Delanie moved from the nursery. The twins were sound asleep. She was happy and content. She gave a little squeal as Don wrapped her into his arms and kissed her. She looked up at him.

"Okay, my love?"

"I am. I love you, Delanie, so much more than yesterday."

The couple was content as they walked back to the kitchen, arms around one another. God had been good. He had been their Defender in their adventure. They would move through life hand in hand and face what He allowed.

———

Thank you for choosing to read the adventures of Don and Delanie, the last of the series about Don's team. It has been a struggle at times to know what to write but they finally shared their story. I will miss him. He has been in many other adventures, even though some of his team were not named in them.

God led them through their adventure, protecting and defending them. He is that for us. He has a plan for our lives that He greatly desires that we follow. We don't always but He knows that we are human. He never leaves us or forsakes us. He only desires what is the best for us.

As to the others who dropped in? Abe's team's story is *His Guardians*. Richard's team is in *His Protectors*. Doug and Darci tell their story in *The Heart of a Lion*. Samuel and his friends are in *His Warriors*. Andrew and Phoebe tell theirs in *The Potter's Hands*. My characters walk back and forth between stories.

May God bless you richly on this journey and adventure called life.

Ronna